A Mercenary's Story

by: Terry Dailey

About the Author

Terry Dailey is a lifelong resident of Alabama. He has traveled extensively, especially within the United States. He boasts, he has visited all 50 states, 6 countries and 2 US territories.

Terry is retired and enjoys reading, writing, working in his shop, cruising the Tennessee River and spending time with friends. Most days he and his dog April, can be found on his boat, the *"Lady J"*.

Though not his first book, **A Mercenary's Story** is Terry Dailey's first action novel. The novel is a fictional writing. As a Vietnam veteran, Terry was able to tap into his military experiences.

Terry started writing at an early age. A composition of these earlier writings and other anecdotal stories are in his book: ***"The Literary World of a Simple Man."*** A copy can be purchased through Amazon.com.

Acknowledgements

Brenda Thorpe. Brenda, I truly appreciate all the work you've put into producing this book. I especially appreciate your encouragement and the occasional "kick in the butt" to keep me going. You are a very special friend.

Cover Artwork: Isabella Dailey - Love you sweetie.

Shere Donofrio. Shere read the first draft of the manuscript. It was her "Thumbs Up" that made me want to finish. She makes great biscuits and gravy.

Carolann Butts. Carolann, you are an inspiration. Your giggles light up a cloudy day, in ways you don't realize.

Technical and Military Advisors

Charles Donofrio, Captain, USMC
Infantry, Vietnam
Pilot, OV-10A Bronco
Captain of the Yacht, *"At Ease"*
Chuck, thanks for all the technical information and advice.
Chuck and I met after I arrived at the Guntersville, Al marina. He became my boating mentor.

Stephen Entrekin, Battlefield Hospital Corpsman HM2 USN
Captain of the Yacht, *"Knot on Call"*
Doc, thanks for all the help and encouragement.
Steve and I grew up in the same area, went to the same high school, graduated the same year. The odd twist: he and I never met until we were both old men.

Table of Contents

Introduction
Chapter 1- Colonel Mathews
Chapter 2 - A Friendship Begins
Chapter 3 - The Team Arrives
Chapter 4 - TET 1968
Chapter 5 - Tracy
Chapter 6 - Invitation
Chapter 7 - Protest
Chapter 8 - Fall in Love
Chapter 9 - The Meeting
Chapter 10 - Standing up the President
Chapter 11 - Escaping
Chapter 12 - Briefings and Gearing Up
Chapter 13 - Career Gone
Chapter 14 - Funeral
Chapter 15 - Shooting
Chapter 16 - MOH
Chapter 17 - New Career
Chapter 18 - Hospital Visits
Chapter 19 - Leaving Town
Chapter 20 - Rehabilitation
Chapter 21 - The Team
Chapter 22 - The Mission Begins
Chapter 23 - Mission Changes
Chapter 24 - Rescue
Chapter 25 - Going Home

Mer-ce-nar-y

NOUN:
1. One who serves or works merely for monetary gain;
2. A hireling.
A professional soldier hired for service in a foreign army.
The American Heritage Dictionary.

Introduction

Mercenaries typically carry an odious reputation. An old European saying I once heard stated: "Every soldier needs three peasants: one to give up his lodging, one to provide for his wife and the third to take his place in Hell". Yet the use of mercenaries is in the history of almost every advanced society. Without them, Carthage could never have challenged Rome.

Mercenaries, though underrated, were a crucial element of medieval warfare. By the end of the medieval period, mercenaries were everywhere in Europe. The Swiss had their famed pikemen, in Italy there were the Italian condottieri, Britain used German Hessian soldiers in the American revolution. The use of mercenaries even spread to Asia where a Turkish General revolted and a group of military men nearly brought down the T'ang dynasty in China.

Most rulers simply found it convenient to use mercenaries. But the era of mercenaries ended drastically during the French Revolution where the entire Swiss Guard was massacred in Paris. This gave birth to a new, modern concept: National sovereignty. National sovereignty required the use of the non-state military activity to cease. Any foreign nationals would be trained, uniformed and officered as units of the national army.

True mercenaries reappeared in the 1960s when new African States lacked a local military infrastructure and briefly employed such troops. A soldier of fortune's dream! What a time it was. And what a selection of soldiers there were to choose from. The war in Southeast Asia had produced a group of excellent soldiers, not only from the United States, but also from Russia, Australia, Korea, Britain and France. These soldiers could be found fighting in any world conflict or third world rebellion from Afghanistan to Cambodia, Honduras to Nicaragua, Ghana to Zaire, with no regard to political ideology, supporting whichever side was willing to pay. At first it was adventurous but not very profitable. Then the drug lords got involved using their seemingly endless wealth to buy and control countries. These cocaine kingpins started hiring modern day gunslingers. Soldiers went from mercenaries to hired assassins to cold blooded killers. Those that didn't have a taste for murder slowly filtered out of existence.

The demand for modern day mercenary armies is no more and probably never will be again. There still remains a small group of us misplaced misfits searching for the ever-elusive dream. We feel we have lost something somewhere, although we no longer know what it is or where it might be.

A few former mercenaries were employed by various government agencies. The one most widely known in the United States is The Central Intelligence Agency, the CIA. A soldier generally served under a contract with the CIA for one year. During this period, he could be sent anywhere at any time. He could not be used for any operation in the territory of the US.☒ A soldier always retained the option to refuse an assignment but was required to attend the assignment meeting. A refusal usually resulted in the soldier being dropped and his contract voided. For this obligation they were paid a yearly salary in addition to a mission fee.

It was through such an arrangement that I met Colonel Joseph Mathews. Retired from the U.S Army, former Green Beret, Airborne Ranger, four tours of Southeast Asia, one silver star, three army commendations, two bronze stars, two purple hearts and currently serving as the CIA Operations Chief in Central America. "The Colonel" as most people knew him, could strike fear in the hearts of men who didn't know the meaning of the word fear.

Chapter 1 - Colonel Mathews

The moment I heard the car turn off the main road onto the dirt driveway leading to my house I knew who it was and why they were coming to see me. I also knew what my answer to their question would be.

I built a house on a small tract of land in the backwoods of Alabama. The house was located on a hill overlooking a small lake. I purposely built the house in the dead center of eight acres of property. I don't want neighbors. I like my privacy. I planned for this house to be my retirement residence. But the boredom of retirement quickly made me realize I was not the retiring type.☒ Though I'm not quite sure what is left for me to do.

The driveway is long. I walked out to the porch and watched the car make the weave around a few small curves and start the ascent up the steep hill to the house. I didn't have the driveway paved and never intend to. A rocky, steep, dirt driveway discourages visitors. I don't like neighbors and I don't like visitors.

I walked to the end of the porch and watched as two men stepped out of the car. It was obvious they had driven all night. They looked tired, clothes wrinkled, hair tousled. Squinting his eyes from the glare of the morning sun, the driver looked up and said, "Is your name Byron Allison?"

"Who wants to know?" I asked. I always like to play their little games. It makes them feel important. The humorous part of all this is that they know who I am and I know who they are.

"Colonel Joseph Mathews said we would find Byron Allison at this location. Are you Mr. Allison?"

By the tone of his voice and the sour expression on his face it was obvious he was not excited over this assignment.

"Yes, I am Byron Allison." A person would have thought my name possessed a sort of magical power. The sheer mention of my name changed the atmosphere. Their facial expressions almost became friendly – almost!

"The Colonel wants you in New Orleans by 8 o'clock tonight," said the driver. "You are booked on the 3 o'clock flight out of Birmingham International Airport and we are here to see that you make that flight."

So much for the friendly expressions, I thought.

"It's not necessary for two overpaid rent-a-cops to act as my bon voyage party," I said.

Sour-face spoke up and said, "Let me make myself clear, Mr. Allison. We are here to see you board that plane. Do you understand?"

There was never any doubt about me going to New Orleans. When the Colonel requests your presence, you comply; if not willingly, then otherwise. I should know. I once chose to decline an invitation. I am still not sure what happened but two days later I woke up in the Colonel's house.

"You gentlemen can relax," I said. "I have every intention of being on that flight." My two personal escorts made sure I boarded the plane bound for New Orleans. I wondered what the Colonel had in store for me since I had been out of touch for over a year. I was curious who else would be in New Orleans. I tried not to admit it but the thought of going back into service excited me.

Shortly after I was discharged from the Army, I was introduced to Colonel Mathews by Senator Dial from California, who was a friend of Clay McLelland and his family. Dial was chairman of the Senate Intelligence Committee. It was in this position that resulted in Dial's and Mathews' relationship.

He was straight forward in his description of what would be expected, should I decide to join his team. Having recently been discharged from the Army and being unemployed, his offer was tempting. However, Senator Dial had offered me a position within his organization as head of his personal security team. In other words, a body guard. I gave both offers considerable thought and decided being a bodyguard would be much safer than becoming a soldier of fortune. Was I ever wrong about that!!

9

As the plane taxied away from the terminal, my mind drifted back to the last time I saw Colonel Mathews. Since I don't remember the actual trip, my memory begins with waking up. The first thing I saw was his cold blue eyes staring at me over the rim of his glasses.

"Byron, my friend," Colonel Mathews said, "I am truly disappointed in you. I am told it was quite an ordeal getting you here. I don't understand the fuss. You know the procedures better than anyone. You are under no obligation to do anything you don't want to. All we ask is that you meet with us occasionally to discuss and possibly advise us on a given operation."

"Yes, I know," I said. "But when have I ever refused?"

"We both know you never have," Mathews snapped back. "That's why I was so surprised to learn it took five agents to get you here."

"What do you mean five agents?" I almost shouted. "I only saw two."

"That would have been Agent Barrett and Agent Curtis," Mathews said sarcastically. He had risen from his seat and walked over to the bar to fix a drink.

"For your information they will be released from the hospital today I am told. The other three agents sedated you and brought you to me.⏹Here," he said, handing me a glass. "Drink this. It will make you feel better."

I took a sip. Cognac, a gentleman's drink. As I drank this high class "rot gut" I thought about how easy it is to toast life today and destroy it tomorrow.

"OK, you have me here, now what?" I said somewhat arrogantly. "What can I do to be of service to your organization?"

"Well, you can lose the attitude for starters" Mathews said, with a bit of an attitude himself. "We all have a job to do and I would prefer all my people to have an open mind and keep their personal problems to themselves. He continued, "However you must put it behind you. I know it must be hard, but if you don't it will totally consume you and everyone around you. I can't take a chance on you not being at one hundred percent. A mental mistake on your part could easily compromise an operation and jeopardize the lives of the members of the team. That's not a risk I'm willing to take."

"Are you cutting me loose?" I asked. I knew he was right in the point he was trying to make.

"That's a decision only you can make," Mathews stated rather firmly. "But you will not be hearing from me again until I'm convinced you are back to being the person I've come to admire and respect."

We sat in silence for a few minutes, each in our own world of thought. The only sounds to be heard were the ticking of the old grandfather clock sitting in the corner and the rattling of the ice in our drink glasses.

The silence was broken when Colonel Matthew spoke up. "Byron, I want you to go back home and decide what you want to do with the remainder of your life. You are, or were, the best Recon Team leader I've ever had. You knew your job and you did it well. You have my number. If I don't hear from you, then I will know your decision."

Colonel Mathews stood and walked toward the door. I rose and followed. He opened the door, and extending his hand he said, "There's a car waiting to take you to the airport. Take care Byron and I hope to hear from you soon."

I shook his hand and walked out.

Chapter 2 - A Friendship Begins

"Sir? Sir? It was the gentle nudge from the stewardess that made me realize I had fallen asleep. I opened my eyes and for a brief moment I thought I was in Heaven. I was gazing into the eyes of an angel. Her beautiful smile reminded me of someone I knew in another life.

"Sir, please fasten your seatbelt," she said. "We will be landing in New Orleans in ten minutes." Apparently, the expression on my face gave my thoughts away. I noticed a slight reddish glow on her face as she walked away. As much as I wanted to ask her to dinner or at least find out her name, I knew there would be little time for socializing in the next few days.

I made my way through the crowded airport, all the while wondering how many times I had made this trip. After a while all airports look identical. But the procedure never changes. I fly to a prearranged location where someone will meet me at the baggage claim, pick me up and take me to a hotel. Rounding the corner on my way to baggage claims, I see an all too familiar sight. Standing next to the baggage conveyor and talking to my beautiful airline stewardess, is Clay McLelland. Clay has a reputation for being a "ladies' man." I could tell he is doing all he can to keep that reputation alive.☒ I casually walked past them to the conveyor and picked up my bag. I know how Clay's mind works and I would bet that he is shooting her a line of bullshit a mile long. Far be it from me to interrupt.

Realizing that he cannot let me stand there forever, Clay jots her number down on a piece of paper.☒ Satisfied that he has done all the damage he can for now, Clay gives her one last flashing smile before heading my way.

Clay McLelland and I go back to the early days of the Vietnam War. I had only been in the country a few weeks when Clay arrived. Both of us were green, dumb, and full of piss and vinegar. We were raised on John Wayne movies and had this "good guy, bad guy" concept of war. It was a well-defined concept of war in which the good guy always triumphs. That concept did not last long.

It was the Army's policy at the time to take new arrivals and team them up with an experienced Non-Commissioned Officer and send them out on a semi-safe patrol. The squad of enlisted men and officers would spend a day in the field getting a feel for the lay of the land while getting some "on the job" training and learn from that experienced NCO. Rank on this patrol meant very little and a good officer recognized this fact and followed the direction of the assigned NCO.

Sergeant Decker was assigned to lead our group and to teach us the things that in the long run could save our lives. Decker was a Master Sergeant and army through and through. He was trained "old school" and boasted his first taste of combat was with Jeb Stuart in the Civil War and he had not missed one since. Out in the field, rank meant nothing to Sergeant Decker. If you screwed up, he would chew your ass out and it did not make any difference whether you were a Private or a Colonel. It was Decker's job to make sure that everyone stayed alive and he was good at what he did.

My first encounter with Sergeant Decker was memorable. The officer's briefing I attended that morning ended late, so consequently I was about three minutes late getting to the assembly area for our first patrol. The two choppers scheduled to take us to our assigned patrol area were sitting on the pad with their engines idling. Sergeant Decker was checking the other members' equipment when I stepped out of the jeep. Not bothering to look up, Decker spoke up in his normal loud gravelly voice.

"Mister Allison, in this man's army you are an Officer and as such, you are the ranking man and entitled to the respect and courtesy as outlined in the Soldier's Handbook. However, on this patrol, you are nothing more than cannon fodder and I expect my cannon fodder to be on time every time, do I make myself clear?"

All branches of the military have a very rigid chain of command and the US Army is no exception. An enlisted man can be court martialed for talking to an Officer in a disrespectful manner, even an old Master Sergeant like Decker. In this case, I understood what Decker was doing and why he was doing it. Decker was charged with the task of taking eight enlisted men ranging from 18 to 20 years old plus two Officers not much older, on a patrol into enemy territory. With the exception of himself, Sergeant Decker knew not one member of this group had any live combat experience. By chastising me in front of the others, Sergeant Decker had established himself as the leader of this patrol. Everyone knew if things got hot Sergeant Decker was the man to follow and that included me too.

"Sorry Sergeant," I said. "I assure you that it won't happen again."

Decker stood, turned to face me, winked and a quick smile flashed across his face. Turning back around, he started issuing orders.

"Lieutenant McLelland, take four men and get their skinny asses on the second chopper. The remaining four get on the first chopper with me and Lieutenant Allison. If anybody needs to take a piss, tough shit, it's game time boys, so you might as well piss on yourself now, cause you're probably going to anyhow.:

Damn, I thought as we boarded the chopper, this man sure has a way with words. Little did most of us know but as the chopper lifted off, our life as we knew it was about to change.

"This ain't no body bag parade!" Sergeant Decker shouted just before the chopper touched down and we all bailed out.

The first couple of hours our patrol was uneventful. Just the type of patrol a person wanted to take a bunch of untested greenies on. We quickly realized Sergeant Decker knew his stuff. He was quick to point out potential booby traps and ambush sites. At one point he set us up in an ambush position and explained the importance of an effective field of fire. These were things we learned in basic training, but now it was the real thing.

Clay was on point and we had just started crossing a waist deep creek when they hit us. It was a small group, probably a patrol just like us. Clay and two others had just reached the top of the far bank when the first round of small arms hit a boy from New York in the face. He never knew what hit him. The impact of the bullet caused his head to explode like an overripe tomato, blowing blood and brain matter all over the guy behind him. That guy went berserk and turned to run, colliding with the guy behind him, causing even more confusion. Sergeant Decker, knowing we had to get across the creek or risk losing Clay and the other guys on the opposite side, waded out in the water with no regard for his own personal safety, screaming and cussing at us like a madman. One of our guys took a round in the arm. Decker grabbed him and got the column moving in the right direction. Carrying the wounded soldier on his shoulder, he was shouting orders and firing his M-16 at the same time.

I don't know if it was the cover fire that Clay and the other two were laying down or the fear of Sgt Decker's threats, but we managed to get across the creek and up the bank without losing anyone else. Once the initial shock was over, we started performing like soldiers. Decker positioned us so a field of fire could be effectively executed. Just as fast as it started, it stopped.

"Byron, you and Clay take the point. Be careful. Look for any bodies or blood trail." Sgt Decker did not have to tell me to be careful. About twenty meters from our position, we found the body. Clay and I stopped and waited for the column to catch up.

The wounded soldier was not Viet Cong like we expected. Rather he was a North Vietnamese Army officer. He had been hit in the mid-section. If there are different degrees of death, a stomach wound has to be the worst way to die. The officer was not dead yet but not far from it. Flies and ants were already on his guts that lay in the dirt.

Decker's face was a bit pale as he stared at the dying NVA officer. I know it was not the sight of a dying man that made Decker's face lose color. This man had seen death in every imaginable form. It had to be something else.

"What is it, Sarge?" I asked.

"I must be getting too old for this," he said. When I look at that dying soldier, I see myself. I think this will be my last war." He paused.

I wasn't sure if he was reflecting on his thoughts or trying to remove the thoughts from his mind.

"We'd better get our asses out of here and fast," he said, now sounding like the commanding sergeant he was. "There's not supposed to be any NVA in this area. We have stumbled into something too big for this motley group to handle. You can bet that after their officer got hit, they broke off to get reinforcements. They want to make damn sure we do not get out of here alive. We must get to the landing zone. G-2 military intelligence will want to know about the NVA in this area." Decker motioned for the radioman to come up.

"Collins, get on the radio," Decker ordered. "Tell HQ to get choppers headed this way. We may not be able to get to the assigned pick-up point. Tell them we will radio our position as they get closer and to expect a hot LZ."

We searched the now dead NVA officer. We didn't find much, a few papers, a letter and a picture of his family. Sergeant Decker began making sure that everyone was spread out. He knew they were going to hit us with mortar and the last thing we needed was to be bunched into one small area.

I don't think Decker even heard the mortar round. Clay and I had taken the point when the round hit at the back of the column. Decker was trying to keep everyone alive. The shell landed about five feet behind him. Call it premonition, call it chance, but he was right, this was his last war.

Being the senior ranking man, I knew it was my job to get us out of there. The NVA had our position zeroed in and the mortar rounds were starting to take their toll. Collins got hit in the leg. The wound was not life-threatening but it would slow us down. Clay grabbed Collins under the arm and started toward a tree line about fifty meters east of our position. The mortars had stopped now. We were firing into the elephant grass-covered terrain in anticipation of a forthcoming ground attack. I ordered everyone except the two guys on the M-60 machine gun and myself to fall back to the tree line. I prayed we could hold back the attackers long enough for everyone to reach Clay and Collins.

I never saw who threw that grenade but I saw it sail over the top of the grass and land near the machine gun crew. All I could do was roll to my left and hope for the best. The concussion of the blast was deafening. I saw the machine gun crew lifted about three feet in the air. Their bodies dropped back to earth in a grotesque manner. A NV soldier jumped up. He could not have been more than twenty feet from me. I squeezed off three quick rounds splitting his chest wide open. I rolled again to my left just as I saw the ground erupt where I had been lying. If I stayed where I was it was just a matter of time before I got hit but if I moved, I was a goner. I decided to take my chances and move, when I heard firing on my right. Then I saw Clay with the other M-60 firing into the grass to our front. Pulling a grenade from his webbing, he tossed it about thirty feet into the enemy position. It was only after I heard the poof of the smoke grenade and saw the red stream of smoke did I realize what was taking place.

"Stardust Two, this is Stardust One," said the chopper pilot over the radio. "I have visual of red smoke. Making a hot approach. Follow me. And remember, we have friendlies on our right side. Over."

As the two gunships started firing their rockets, I motioned to Clay and we started to fall back to the tree line. I could hear the chopper's rockets exploding on impact and felt the heat and concussion from the blasts. I don't know how anything could survive this mayhem of hell.

But survive they did. As Clay and I ran towards the tree line, I could see the grass shredding apart as the hot lead, fired by the NVA, sailed past us. We reached the tree line at the exact same moment. Diving for cover behind a fallen tree, we collided in midair, our bodies bouncing off one another. I hit the ground breathless but otherwise unhurt. I rolled and came up just in time to see three enemy soldiers coming through the grass following the path Clay and I had made. I fired, hitting the first one just above the knees, severing one leg and mangling the other. Clay caught the second, sending him into a back flip. The third soldier tried to turn and retreat but a blast of automatic fire caught him in midstride, splattering the surrounding grass with blood.

Because of the deadly concentration of fire we were doling out and the havoc caused by the gunships overhead, the attackers broke off and started pulling back.

"Land Rover. Land Rover. This is Stardust One. Do you read? Over." It took me a second to realize that they were calling us over the radio.

"Stardust One, this is Land Rover! Over!" I shouted.

"Land Rover there is a clearing about twenty-five meters to the north of your position. Have your people fall back to that point and pop smoke for extraction. Over."

"Roger that, Stardust. Will do!" I was still shouting, though not sure why. "And thanks."

"Roger that, Land Rover. Glad we could be of assistance," the pilot said calmly. "Just doing our job. Out."

I made a mental note to look that guy up and buy him the biggest, coldest beer in Vietnam. Turning to Clay, I told him the plan.

"Okay, we are falling back, Take point." I directed Clay. "And scout out the clearing north of here. Everyone else, stay low, but fall back. Be careful.⯑ We are too close to getting out of here to screw up now."

I said that last part to myself more than to anybody else.

"Get the wounded and move back first."

I took the radio from the now wounded Collins and we started our move as instructed by the chopper pilot.⯑As we moved, we could still hear the gunships raining down a hell of gunfire. Once we reached the clearing, I pulled the pin from a smoke grenade and tossed it.

The radio crackled. "Land Rover this is Pied Piper. We are your ride home. Copy?☐"

"Pied Piper this is Land Rover. Good to hear you. Over."

"Land Rover I have visual on smoke. Please Identify. Over."

"Roger, Pied Piper. Smoke Yellow. I repeat Smoke Yellow. Over."

The enemy has a bad habit of setting off smoke grenades to try and lure unsuspecting choppers into an ambush. Verifying the color of the smoke through the radio was necessary to thwart the enemy's plan to shoot down our choppers.

"Roger, Land Rover" said the pilot. "Have your people ready. Don't want to be down long. ETA is two minutes. Over and out."

The chopper didn't have to worry about being on the ground very long. We were ready. Clay and I were the last ones to board, after loading our wounded.

Once we gained enough altitude to feel safe, I looked over at Clay. He was sitting across from me with that shit-eating smile he is so famous for. He reached in his pocket and pulled out a pack of bent, twisted cigarettes. I leaned and took the pack from his hand, pulled two out, lit one and handed it to him.☐ After lighting mine I took a deep breath. A person can thank someone in many different ways but there are no words to describe the gratitude you feel when someone has saved your life. I handed back the pack of cigarettes, nodded my head and said thanks. Clay took a draw of his cigarette, cocked his head and smiled. No other words were necessary. He knew what I meant and how I felt. I knew I had a friend for life.

Chapter 3 - The Team Arrives

After getting my bag, I hailed a cab, and Clay and I started our ride to the hotel.

"When did you get here?" I asked.

"I arrived this morning," he said. "I don't know when the others got here."

"Who's all here?" I asked.⬛ The C8olonel is famous for being able to pick the right people for the job. I had a feeling I knew who would be waiting at the hotel before Clay even answered the question.

"I saw Tom Brookfield checking in as I was leaving to meet you at the airport," he said. "Tony Danley and KP Carroll were in the hotel bar. And I heard the desk clerk page Cliff Rush, though I never actually saw him."

As Clay was naming these people, I realized that this small group was the cream of the crop of former military men. These, and about eight or ten others were the best trained "Behind the lines" operators in the entire world.

⬛Two former operators had been killed about six months ago while doing some freelance work in South Africa as mercenaries. The Colonel tries to discourage such activities. A freelance operator never really knows and usually does not care who he is working for as long as the money justifies the risk. The operator does the job he is paid to do and as is the case sometimes, he is fighting against the very people that may be his employer next month.⬛ Merely a gun-for-hire, getting killed is just an occupational hazard. The Colonel views it as a waste of money. I view it as a waste, period.⍰ I realized Clay was still talking to me though I hadn't been listening.

"I saw a big fellow in the lobby," Clay said. "I didn't recognize him. He looked like he was waiting on someone. He really stood out. I've never seen a bigger man in my life. He had arms bigger than my leg," Clay continued. "But the strangest thing about him wasn't his size, but the look in his eyes. He had a stare that could bend cold steel."

I knew exactly who Clay was talking about. If you had ever met this man, you'd never forget him either.⍰ Howard Andrews was his name and he was about the meanest son-of-a-bitch I've ever met.

Howard enlisted in the Marine Corps at the age of seventeen. The juvenile court in his hometown of Pittsburgh, Pennsylvania, gave him a choice: enlist in the Marines, or serve a five-year prison sentence.⍰ The judge did Pittsburgh a great favor though many Marines hated his decision.

Called 'Hal' by his friends, though he didn't have many, Hal made it through basic training without very much trouble. During his tour of Vietnam, the highest rank Hal ever held was Lance Corporal. Twice he was promoted and twice he was busted. The longest he ever held Lance Corporal was two weeks. The way the story was told, Hal and another Marine, both of them half-drunk, got into an argument over who was the meanest Marine in the Corps.⍰ The unlucky Marine made the mistake of calling Hal a "nigger." Before enough Marines could subdue him, Hal had almost beaten the other Marine to death. The second time Hal was busted was for striking an officer and breaking his jaw. Hal was court martialed and spent six months in the Long Bien Jail in Long Bien, Vietnam.

In the field he was a flawless soldier. He was a small arms specialist and had no equal when it came to hand-to-hand combat. In the rear echelon area, he was a live grenade without the pin. Hal loved drinking and fighting and hated officers. At six-foot-eight, he was three hundred and fifty pounds of pure soldier. Hal had to be the meanest human being to ever shit between a pair of boots.

The cab pulled up in front of the hotel. I reached down to get my bag from the floorboards. Clay paid the driver as I stepped from the cab. I looked up at the hotel. The sign read 'St. Charles.' In her day, the 'St. Charles' was a grand hotel. Like so many other grand old places, time has passed by the 'St Charles.' The Colonel and his CIA-backed organization picked out-of-the-way places just like this on purpose. Wherever we are boarded, you can bet it's only a step above skid-row and well below the status of the Ritz-Carlton. Everything always follows the same procedure. We all fly in from different locations but we're all put in the same hotel. While we're there we do not socialize with each other or with any of the locals. Each member of the team tries to draw as little attention to himself as possible. You wait until you are contacted then follow whatever instruction you are given.

The lobby of the hotel was mostly vacant. I could hear some talking and music coming from the hotel bar at the far-right side of the lobby. There was the faint sound of clanking silverware and tinkling of glasses coming from behind the closed doors of the hotel restaurant. There was a bellhop rolling an empty luggage cart toward the elevator. Two people stood behind the front desk. One of the desk clerks smiled as I approached the counter.

"Can I help you?" the desk clerk asked.

"Yes, my name is Byron Allison," I said.

The desk clerk shuffled some papers around. "Certainly Mr. Allison, we have been expecting you. Your room is ready." He handed me the key.

"You also have a message." The clerk laid a folded piece of paper on the counter.

I looked at the key. Room 218. Then unfolded the note. It was a plain piece of white paper with a short-typed message:

8 AM. Out Front. You and Clay.

Short, precise and to the point. That was the Colonel's way whether in person or on paper. The Colonel never changed.

By this time Clay had caught up with me, though I'm not sure where I lost him. I handed the note to Clay. He read it, nodded his head and handed it back.

"Dinner?" he asked.

"No, I think I'll pass." It had been a long day with even longer ones to come. All I wanted was a shower and a good night's sleep.

Clay headed for the restaurant. And I headed for the elevator.

After showering and catching the local news on the TV, I laid down across the bed. I went to sleep thinking about Clay and his family. More specifically about Clay's sister Tracy. It was during me and Clay's second tour of Vietnam when I learned he had a sister. I was shocked to learn of her existence. Clay talked about his father and mother a few times but never mentioned a sister. I knew Clay's family owned an electronics manufacturing company in Southern California. I knew they supplied the government with electronic components for the guidance system of some sophisticated, classified missile. I also knew Clay's father was big in the "behind the scenes" political world in California. And this is how I found out Clay was being groomed for political greatness within his home state. With their money and political connections, it was not beyond the realm of possibility that Clay could become governor of California.

All this I knew before I knew he had a sister. Two years his junior, it seems Tracy was as strong-willed as the rest of the family. On this particular day, Clay had received a letter from his mother. In this letter, Clay's mother told him that his sister was arrested during a demonstration at the University of California in Berkeley, California. Tracy was a political activist, demonstrating against the very war her brother was fighting in. What Tracy stood against was the very thing the rest of the family stood for. Clay explained that neither he nor his father criticized Tracy for doing what she believed so strongly in. Like Clay, she was raised to be a "self-thinker."

She was encouraged to follow her own set of beliefs regardless of what side of the line those beliefs fell on. Clay did say, his mother made sure their house was "neutral territory" and refused to allow debates between Tracy and her father. This helped keep peace in the family and harmony at home.

I'm not sure how long I'd been asleep, but it couldn't have been more than a couple of hours. I awoke to the same feeling I had awakened on so many nights over so many years. I could feel the warmth from her body and smell the fragrance of her perfume. Even though I know she's not there, the urge to reach out and touch her soft skin is so overwhelming I can't resist the temptation. Sometimes I would pull a pillow up close to my chest in hopes I could go back to sleep and for a brief moment, convince my sub-conscience that she's lying beside me. It rarely ever worked. One never truly knows how bad they can miss something until it's gone. At some point I always drift back to sleep. The sweet smell of her sheer essence still lingers on my mind. My feelings for her cannot be denied and my memories of her will not be forgotten.

Chapter 4 - TET 1968

During my second tour of duty in Vietnam, I commanded Charlie Company of the 536th Light Infantry Brigade. At the time Charlie Company was housed in an old rice mill located on the edge of the Mekong Delta in Cholon, Vietnam.

For an Infantry outfit, our accommodations were not bad. Unlike the remainder of the 536th, we didn't live in tents and sleep in mud. Our billet area was an old warehouse with a roof made of slate tiles. We even had makeshift "showers." The showers were supplied by a water tank located on top of the building. On very hot days you could get lukewarm water if you were lucky.

The compound was situated on a small island surrounded by a canal that was fed from the Saigon River on one side, and the delta on the other. A bridge on the northern side of the island connected to the mainland and the southern bridge led into the delta.

The main entrance to the compound was off a small road that circled the island. The gate into the compound was flanked by two heavily fortified bunkers that faced the northern bridge. The back side of the camp was surrounded by a twelve-foot-high rock wall built by the French during their occupation. This wall offered some protection from sniper fire and acted as a second line of defense in the case of a frontal fire. Strategically located around the wall were six towers looking out over a clearing that separated the base camp from the southern bridge. About 150 yards out from the wall was a semicircle of sandbag bunkers that served as an outer perimeter of defense.

Our primary objective at this location was two-fold. The first to maintain control of both bridges since they were the key to traffic into and out of the Mekong Delta. Our second objective was to run reconnaissance, and search and destroy operations in the delta both to gauge enemy strengths and offer some protection to the villages from enemy insurgencies.

On the Tet holiday of January 30th, 1968, the Chinese lunar year of the Monkey, all hell broke loose. I was six months into my second tour. We had seen signs of increased enemy activity for over a week. We had successfully ambushed Viet Cong patrols on three separate occasions in that one week alone. All three VC patrols had been no more than a mile from our base camp. A squad of VC had ambushed one of our patrols just two nights before this one. The enemy was operating in and around our area and we knew it. No one was getting very much sleep because of it. We knew something was going to happen. We just didn't know what or when.

It was three o'clock in the morning when I received the first call from the radio operator in the command center. I had not gone to bed on this night. Something in my gut told me that this was going to be the night.⏺

"Captain," The radio operator started. "We have reports of troop movement just across the southern bridge."

The words had no more than echoed across my radio headset when I heard the first mortar round explode, followed by a barrage of rounds throughout the compound. As I made my way to the command bunker, I heard automatic gunfire cut loose on our southern flank.

. "Get Lt. McLelland on the radio!" I shouted as I entered the command bunker.

"Got him on the line," said the operator, as he handed me the headset.

"Clay, buy me ten minutes and then start falling back to the inner perimeter, that will give me enough time to reinforce the inner wall and give you people supporting fire. We will make our stand there, over."⏺

"Okay Captain, ten minutes," Clay said. "But eight would be better. Out."

With the size of the force that Clay was facing, I knew I had to get him and his people back into the compound or risk losing them.⏺ While getting a report from the northern sector, I summoned First Sergeant Gonzales.

"First Sergeant," I instructed. "We have First Platoon in the northern sector and Forth Platoon in the southern.⏺ I want you to get Second Platoon to the southern wall and provide support so that Forth Platoon can fall back inside the wall. I will hold Third Platoon in reserve."

"Will do Captain!" Sgt Gonzales snapped as he ran out of the bunker.

I instructed the radio operator to contact Brigade and let them know we were under a full attack by a sizable force.

Sgt Gonzales came rushing back into the bunker, blood running down the side of his face.

"Captain, we have a problem," he exclaimed breathlessly. "When the mortar rounds hit the slate roof, shards of the tiles splintered throughout the billet area like buckshot.⊡ Second and Third Platoons sustained over sixty percent casualties."

It was at that moment that I realized we were in deep shit.

"Okay Sergeant," I said, taking a deep breath and trying to comprehend the situation.

"Take everyone you can muster, walking wounded and all, anyone that can fire a rifle. Get them situated in the southern sector and be fast about it. Lieutenant McLelland and his force will be falling back in about four minutes."

"Will do Captain," said Gonzales as he exited the bunker.

The worst position of any commander is to find himself in a major defensive battle with little or no reserve to fall back on. And I was in just such a position.

"Captain Allison, I have Lieutenant McLelland on the radio," shouted the radio operator.

"Clay, what is your situation?" I asked, half afraid of what his answer might be.

"We have moderate casualties," Clay responded. "But we made it back inside. The bastards have breached the wall in one or two places, but so far, we are holding our own."

"Clay," I said solemnly. "I don't have anyone else to send. You've got to make do with what you have. Hold your position at all costs. The southern sector has been compromised. Tell your people to stay where they're at and shoot anything that moves."

"I understand," Clay said calmly and the radio fell silent.

I turned to look at the map just as the rocket propelled grenade exploded into the side of the bunker. The RPG failed to penetrate the sand bagged wall but the blast and heat knocked me down. Dust hung in the air so thick that visibility was almost non-existent. This was followed by the sound of gunfire outside the bunker. Standing by the bunker's entrance wall, what I saw made my blood run cold. Out in the canal straight across from the main gate was what looked like a miniature navy. Men in small boats were attempting to row across the canal. The machine guns on each side of the main gate were wreaking havoc on the boats and their crews but some were still making it across. The high angle of the canal bank made it impossible for the machine gun to fire at the enemy once they made it to shore, without the machine gunners exposing themselves. I could hear heavy fighting going on in the vicinity of the northern bridge and knew that they were under attack as well. We were being hit on all sides.

I saw one soldier lob a grenade down the canal bank and take a bullet in the chest in the process. With my radio operator in tow, we ran to the right-side main gate bunker. Grabbing the M-60 in one hand and a large ammo can in the other, I instructed the operator

31

to get the other full can. We exited the bunker and ran across the road and dropped behind a small berm not five feet from the canal bank. I pulled three grenades from my web and tossed them down the bank. Once they exploded, we jumped up and opened fire at the enemy up and down the canal.

I felt the bullet when it sliced through my left thigh. The only thing I remember was it burning but when I tried to move, my leg gave way. I turned to my radio operator to give him the M-60 and let him take over, only to realize he had taken a bullet to the head. Propping myself up as best I could, I continued to fire down the bank and across the waterway. I felt a tug at my shirt and a sharp pain in my right shoulder but adrenaline kept me from stopping. I knew if I stopped now, I was a dead man. I continued firing, pausing briefly to reload a new belt of ammunition.

By the time I ran out of ammo in the second belt, I realized the gunfire around was sparse and distant. I was terrified, relieved, excited and tired all at once. And then I passed out.

I remember waking up in the chopper on the way to the hospital. I looked up and there was a medic standing over me holding an IV bag. He looked at me and yelled to be heard over the rotor noise.

"You are going to be alright sir," he said. "You got a couple of nasty wounds, but I got the bleeding under control and we will be at an aid station in a few minutes. Must have been one hell of a fire fight ya'll had back there, dead gooks everywhere. I gave you a shot of morphine and you'll be okay. Don't worry sir."

That's all I remember him saying. He may not have even said that much. I was so out of it from the pain and then the morphine started kicking in. I tried to ask about the others, but couldn't make myself heard over the chopper's noise.

I faded in and out of consciousness for the next few hours. When I awoke, I realized I was in some sort of hospital ward surrounded by cots. I lay there, with my eyes closed, trying to comprehend the events as best I could remember. My right arm was bandaged and strapped to my chest. I tried to move and felt a searing pain on the inside of my upper left leg. Very close to the groin area. I broke out in a cold sweat. How bad had I been hit? Running my left hand down my stomach, I reached for my balls just as a nurse spoke up.

"They're all there, Captain, and unless you are planning on playing with them, I would suggest you remain very still and go back to sleep. The last thing you want is to start the bleeding again."

I opened my eyes and this very tired looking nurse was standing at the foot of my bed holding a clipboard. She smiled and her eyes lit up.

"You guys beat all I've ever seen," she said, still smiling. "It makes no difference how bad a soldier might be shot, the first thing he checks is his family jewels."

"Those are valuable jewels," I said, sounding weaker than I thought I would. "If that's my chart you are holding, please tell me what it says."

"Well, let me see," she said, starting to lose her smile. It says here that you were shot twice, once in the right shoulder and again in the left thigh. But then, I'm not telling you anything you don't already know, am I?" Her smile came back.

"Not really," I said, a little stronger this time. "How bad is it?"

"The one in the thigh didn't hit anything major and caused minimum muscle damage. You'll have a nice scar to show your wife, but it will heal pretty fast." She lost her smile again and had a very serious expression now. "The bullet that went in your shoulder clipped the bone. It will take longer to heal, but should not cause you any problems. If I had to guess," she said. "In three to four weeks you'll be ninety percent or better."

"I don't have a wife," I said, louder than I meant too.

"I don't have a wife to show my scars to," I said trying to muster up a smile.

"Well, I doubt you will find one here." She smiled. "We'll have to get you better and get you out of here so you can find you one." She patted my good shoulder and turned and walked away.

The next morning, I had a visit from our Battalion Commander, Colonel Pardue.

"Well Captain Allison, you and your people had one hell of a night," Pardue stated. "Damn fine job Charlie Company did, holding back the enemy. I don't know if anyone has told you yet, but you were hit by two companies of VC."

"No sir, I haven't spoken with anyone. In fact, I need to find out how bad our casualties were, sir," I said as Pardue pulled up a stool and sat down next to my bed.

"We are not releasing causality numbers at this point," Colonel Pardue said in a low voice. "G2 and the upper brass don't want the North Vietnamese or the press to know how bad we were caught off guard. Hell, if the press gets wind of the numbers, they will straight line the information to Hanoi." Pardue took a deep breath and continued. "However, I can tell you that Charlie Company's kill ratio was about ten to one. And from what information I gathered and saw for myself, you are responsible for that number being so high. In fact, had you not stopped them from crossing the canal, they would have gained control of the main road. According to captured information and statements obtained from some POWs, that road was going to be their main route into and out of Saigon. By depriving them of this road and the north bridge, you kept reinforcements from getting into the city and closed their escape route. That's a damn fine accomplishment for a small company. Hell, Captain, I don't know if you realize it, but had it not been for the heroic action of Charlie Company and yourself the results would have been far worse. The VC your company held back were reinforcements for two companies of VC that breached the wall at the American Embassy. But because their reinforcement didn't make it, they could not sustain their attack." Colonel Pardue stood up and straightened his jacket.

"Captain Allison," he said in a fine military tone. "It's on behalf of General Gavin Hanner, Commanding General of the 536th Light Infantry Brigade, that I have the pleasure to inform you that, as of 0800 hours, you have been recommended for the Congressional Medal of Honor for your action above and beyond the call of duty at Cholon on February 1st 1968." He saluted me.

⁇ Pardue cleared his throat and sat back down on the stool. Almost whispering again, he said, "Charlie Company is back at brigade headquarters for some much-deserved rest and relaxation. This will also give them time to re-fit, and get their reinforcement in place."

Pardue stood up again and speaking a little louder said,

"Byron, we know you will be out of service for at least a few weeks. I've placed Lieutenant McLelland in charge of Charlie Company temporarily.⬚ I hope this meets with your approval.

"Lieutenant McClelland is fine with me, sir," I said. I felt better just knowing Clay was alright. "He's a fine leader and will make a good company commander."⬚

Pardue laid his hand on my left shoulder and said, "Byron, don't give the personnel here at the hospital too hard a time.⬚ Take care of yourself and see me as soon as you are released."

"I will sir." He nodded and turned and walked away.

Chapter 5 - Tracy

My wounds alone were not enough to get me shipped stateside. However, being a recipient of the nation's highest military honor was.

Once it was verified that Congress was going to approve the award, I was ordered back to the States. I wasn't entirely pleased with this action but Medal of Honor awardees were no longer allowed in battle.

It was later explained to me by a Senator in Washington, DC, that it would not be in the best interest of the country to have a recipient of our nation's highest military honor to be killed, or even worse captured in battle. Nothing I could do would prevent me from being shipped back to stateside duty.⬚

Upon receiving the word that I was going stateside Clay insisted I stop off and visit his family. I thought about protesting, but it seemed like a waste of time. Once Clay's family learned that a soldier and friend that fought side-by-side with their son was being awarded the Congressional Medal of Honor, they insisted that I stop for a visit.

Clay's father arranged to have me picked up at the airport, in a limousine no less, driven to their home just outside of Ocean Circle, California. The house was evenmore beautiful than Clay had described. It sat on a cliff overlooking the Pacific Ocean. The long driveway was lined with palm trees, beautiful manicured green lawns surrounded the house. A fountain stood in front of the house, and marble steps leading up to the columned porch. I have never felt more out of place in my life, and I was only in their driveway. The limo drove around the fountain and stopped directly in front of the steps. The driver insisted that he get my bags for me. So, I made my way up the steps and rang the doorbell.

A short, delicate, beautiful woman opened the door. "You must be Byron!" she said. "It is so wonderful to have you here. I'm Sandra McLelland, Clay's mother."

"It's nice to meet you Mrs. McLelland," I said.

I tipped my hat to her, hoping that it was the "gentlemanly" thing to do. It was very obvious to me that Clay did not get his looks from this lovely lady.

"Clayton isn't home yet" she said. "But he will be here shortly. We have a guest room prepared for you. And I hope it's not an imposition, but we have some guests over this evening to a reception in your honor."

This was the first I had heard about a party for me. I tried not to look too shocked but I must not have done a good job.

"Clay didn't tell you that we planned a reception? I told that boy to make sure he told you. Well anyhow, it'll just be a few people that Clayton wants to introduce you to. I'll have our housekeeper show you to your room where you can freshen up."

"Thank you, Mrs. McLelland," I said.

I realized that I hadn't said much. I hoped she didn't think I was rude but I was just tired and overwhelmed.

I barely had time to shower and change before the guests started arriving. To my surprise, my dress uniform was already laid out on the bed. While I was showering, someone had pressed my shirt and shined my shoes.

After dressing, I was escorted into a large elegant room to meet Clay's father, Clayton G. McLelland, Sr. When I entered the room, Clayton sprang from his chair and practically charged across the room.

"Byron," he said, shaking my hand vigorously. "How do you do? Clay has told us so much about you I feel that I have known you for years."

"It's a pleasure to meet you sir," I said. "Thank you for having me. I only wish you hadn't gone through so much trouble to have a reception for me."

"Don't be silly," he said "It is an honor and a pleasure to have you here. It's not often we have such a distinguished military hero in our midst. Besides, you being the decorated war hero that you are, and a friend to my boy, well that certainly can't do Clay any harm politically, can it?" He laughed. "I'm only kidding. I consider you a part of the family already. How about something to drink?" he offered as he walked around the very large, seemingly well-stocked bar in the corner of the room.

"Crown Royal, straight and neat, would be nice," I said.

"Crown, straight and neat it is." He motioned for me to have a seat. He fixed himself a drink and began asking me questions about Clay and his safety. Questions which I answered to the best of my ability without telling him exactly how dangerous Vietnam was, and how you never really knew which breath was going to be your last. I figured he knew it was dangerous enough and I didn't elaborate. Clayton sat down across from me, put an unlit cigar in his mouth and continued talking about Clay.

"You do realize that I plan for Clay to be the governor of California, don't you?" Before I could answer he continued, "Hell, he may even be President." He laughed but we both knew he was serious. Clayton took a deep breath and continued. "Politically, Clay joining the Army was a great move. Volunteering for Vietnam was a risky, but a wise choice. All voters like a veteran. But agreeing to a second tour just does not make sense to me."

"Clay is very capable of taking care of himself," I assured him. "I'm certain that he's one of the best soldiers we've got over there." I left out the fact that Clay had a habit of volunteering for assignments that appear to be dangerous.

Taking the still unlit cigar from his mouth, Clayton leaned forward in his chair. He smiled and asked, "Have you met Tracy yet?"

"No sir," I answered. "I haven't had the pleasure yet."

"You will real soon." Clayton laughed. "Whether it's a pleasure or not depends on your definition of pleasure. She is a very strong-minded young lady. I swear she must've gotten her hard-headedness from her mother's side of the family. If she starts getting to you with her far left-wing political views just remind her that you are our guest and that should shut her up. She knows and respects her mother's feelings about heated debates here in the house."

Clayton stood up, laid his cigar on the side table and reached out and shook my hand. "Come on," he said. "There is a group of people waiting to meet you." I stood up and he put his arm around my shoulder. "These people don't know it yet but they are the future contributors to Clay's political life."

"Clay told me to watch you. He said that every move you make is politically motivated."

Clayton laughed and slapped me on the back. "That boy is smarter than I give him credit for."

We made our way to the dining room where everyone was gathered for the reception. Though dining room wasn't exactly the term I would use to describe this room. Its size rivaled some of the largest mess halls I had eaten in with hundreds of other men at once.

I was expecting twenty, maybe thirty guests. But as I stood at the doorway and couldn't believe what my eyes were seeing. There had to be over 200 people. If this was their idea of "having a few guests over" I'd hate to see what it was like when they decided to throw a big party.

Clayton started introducing me around. I did alright for the first few introductions but then all the names and faces started running together. After meeting twenty people in less than five minutes, I finally decided to stop trying to remember names. I think the whiskey began taking its effect on me. I was tired from the trip and the change in time zones had me in a tailspin. I tried to put on a perky attitude in front of all these people but all I really wanted to do was lie down and sleep for a long time.

And then she walked up! I knew at first sight that this was Tracy McLelland. The family resemblance was too much to ignore, though this was not what I expected her to look like. I had a preconceived mental picture of Tracy; a flower child with long straight hair, bell bottom blue jeans and "make love not war" patches sewn onto her shirt.

Man was I ever wrong! Just the sight of her beauty made my mind and body snap back to life. She was smiling and she walked towards me, her long blond hair flowing around her. She wore a sky-blue dress that matched her eyes perfectly. And her eyes, they sparkled like diamonds. I just stood there spellbound.

My ears were hearing her introduce herself as Tracy McLelland but my eyes were telling my brain that what I was seeing could not possibly be her.

"Excuse me," she said.

I realized that my jaw was lax. I was standing there with my mouth agape. I shut my mouth and prayed to God that I hadn't actually drooled.

"If you would be so kind as to mentally put my clothes back on me, I would appreciate it.

"I'm sorry," I said. "I was just, uhm, I was..." *You bumbling idiot, think of something to say!* My mind was screaming at me.

"I was just thinking..."

"It's blatantly obvious," she interrupted, "what you were thinking."

"I'm sorry." My face was turning redder by the second. "You are not what I expected. I was struggling to regain my composure.

"Okay Mr. Allison," she taunted. "Just exactly what were you expecting?"

I knew I was losing this battle. I was digging myself into a deeper hole with every word.

"I surrender," I said. "You are correct in your assumptions and I humbly apologize. If you will be so forgiving and allow me this one mistake, I will strive never to disappoint you again." *Chivalry works every time,* I thought.

"You are as full of shit as everyone else here" she snapped.

So much for chivalry.

"But," she continued, "in the interest of a peaceful evening I will let it slide."

Realizing that in addition to looking like an idiot, I have made a fool of myself, I tried to sincerely maneuver my way out of this corner I had backed myself into. "You have every right to be angry," I said. "But I have to admit that you are not what I expected. I sincerely apologize."

She smiled and reached down to take my hand.

"Hello, Mr. Allison," she said. "My name is Tracy." She smiled. "And I accept your apology, Besides, I couldn't stay mad at a friend of Clay's for very long."

"It's nice to meet you, Tracy," I said. "And you can call me Byron." She squeezed my hand and smiled, and I breathed a sigh of relief.

"It's nice to meet you, Tracy," I said. "And you can call me Byron." She squeezed my hand and smiled, and I breathed a sigh of relief.

"How is Clay?" she asked.

"Clay was doing fine when I last saw him," I answered.

"So, I understand you're a big war hero," she said.

"I don't see myself as a big war hero," I said. "I was just doing my job and trying to stay alive at the same time. In fact, if it was up to me, I'd still be over there doing that job. But after seeing you I am glad..."

"Byron my boy!" Clayton walked up and interrupted me. I had never been so relieved, I realized I was about to embarrass myself again. What is it about beautiful women that brings the fool out in a man?

"Byron," Clayton said. "I must introduce you to Senator Joseph Dial. Doesn't this boy look sharp? I tell you; you are looking at the future of America, right? This boy is on his way to greatness."

I halfheartedly shook the Senator's hand and tried to seem interested in the conversation going on but I was more concerned with watching Tracy out of the corner of my eye. The Senator was saying something about the country being proud of men like myself. I thanked him and tried to make eye contact with him and act sincere, but I had lost sight of Tracy. She had disappeared into the throng of people.⍰ *I really blew it.* I was thinking. *I'll never see her again.*

I shook several more hands but made no attempt to remember names. I felt like the life had been sucked right back out of my body. And again, I felt like sleeping. And then I felt the lightest tap on my shoulder. I turned around and found myself looking into the sky-blue eyes of Tracy. I was shocked back to life. She slipped a note in my hand and before I could say anything, she disappeared so quickly that I wondered if she had been there at all or if I was hallucinating from lack of sleep. Then I realized I was holding a note. I turned back around and saw Clayton engrossed in a conversation with a few other people so I slipped away unnoticed to the first quiet corner I could find.

I unfolded the note and it said:

If you are as tired of shaking hands as you look, meet me around front in fifteen minutes.

These people are too involved in their own self-worth to miss us.

Tracy

P.S. Change clothes – no uniform please.

It didn't take me long to find my way back upstairs to my room and change into my civilian clothes. I made my way back downstairs and walked right past the reception completely unnoticed. Without the uniform it seemed like I was invisible. I walked out onto the front steps just as Tracy drove up in a 1968 metallic blue Corvette Stingray Convertible. The white interior was pristine and the top was down.

"Hurry up and get in," she said, "before someone sees us."

We drove for a while without either saying a word. Finally, I broke the silence.

"Why no uniform?" I asked. She looked at me, puzzled. "Your note said no uniform. I was just wondering why."

"Oh!" she said. "I have to protect my reputation." She laughed. "After all, I am an anti-war activist. How would it look for me to be seen in public with a highly decorated army officer?" She paused and glanced at me. "Besides, you don't strike me as a button collar and tie man. I figured you would be more comfortable in normal clothes."

"I appreciate your concern," I said. "You are right about being more comfortable. That uniform starts to itch after a while. Plus, I would not want to compromise your reputation as an anti-war activist."

We both laughed.

Damn, I thought. *She is pretty when she laughs.*

We drove along in silence again for a few more miles. I watched the sun set and the rays reflect off the ocean. We entered a small town. Tracy slowed and stopped as the lights turned red. This small town reminded me of back home. For some reason, when I thought of California, I thought of big cities and beaches. But this town was almost like home.

Tracy broke the silence this time. "Does the Army pay you enough to buy me an expensive dinner or do I need to start looking for a burger joint?"

Before I could respond she interjected, "I know what we'll do." The light turned green and she gassed it. "Let's go to the country club. You and I there together will give those old goats something to talk about. We'll put dinner on Daddy's tab. He'd never forgive me if I let you pay."

We drove up the front drive of the Stone Hedge Country Club. Tracy stopped the car right in front of the doors. Two attendants came to the car and opened our doors.

"Good evening, Miss McLelland," the man opening Tracy's door said.

"Good evening, Sam," she said. She handed him the car keys. "Take care of it for me, will you?"

"Sure thing, Miss," he said.

The front entrance to the country club was immense. Stairs led up to the covered porch supported by four giant marble columns. Two doormen opened the massive doors. Stone Hedge Country Club smelled of money. Big Money, lots more money than I'd ever have.

The manager greeted us when we entered the foyer.

"Good evening, Miss McLelland," he said. His tone oozed fake and his smile was forced.

"It's so nice to have you with us this evening." I detected sarcasm in his voice. Turning his attention to me, he continued. "Good evening, sir. My name is James Farland." He extended his hand and I shook it.

"Glad to meet you, Mr. Farland," I said. "My name is Byron Allison."

"Well Mr. Allison, I trust you and Miss McLelland will find our modest accommodations adequate. Enjoy your evening."

We turned and started down the long corridor.

"Could you tell he didn't like me?" Tracy asked. I turned to make sure we were out of earshot of Mr. Farland. If he had heard her, he didn't give any indication. He was absorbed in paperwork at the front desk.

"Yeah," I said. "It was obvious. What's his problem?"

"I may have offended him," she said.

"May have?" I questioned, hoping to squeeze a better answer out of her. I was intrigued.

"Well Daddy hosted a fundraiser here at the county club for Senator Dial's re-election," she began.

"Senator Dial?" The name rang a bell. "Didn't I meet him tonight?"

"Yes, you did," she said. "He and Daddy are very good friends. And he is a very big supporter of the war. So, there was a fundraiser and I may have told a few fellow war protesters about it."

"Wait a minute," I said, stopping in the middle of the corridor. "You're telling me that you organized a demonstration outside an event hosted by your father at his country club, to protest against his best friend who happens to be a pro-war senator?"

"Don't make it sound so bad!" she said. "I didn't organize it. I just provided the information to someone else to organize. But to James Farland, I might as well have organized a protest in his own backyard. He took it way too personally. Anyone else he would have banned from the country club grounds, but because of my father being, well, my father, Mr. Farland still has to let me in those doors."

I laughed. "You are really something, you know that, don't you?"

She smiled at me. "Come on," she said, tugging at my arm. "Let's get to the dining room, I'm starving!"

Our entrance into the dining room did not go unnoticed. We were seated under the watchful eyes of, at my best count, about fifteen other people. A few couples scattered around the outer edges of the room and two groups of four or five seated at the larger tables in the middle.

"I can feel these people watching me," I whispered to Tracy as she sat down in the chair that I pulled out for her. "Their eyes are boring holes into me."

"It's not you they're boring holes into," she said. "It's me. Most of Daddy's friends and associates view me as an embarrassment."

We sat in silence for a few moments as we each contemplated the menu choices. There were things on this menu that I didn't even know you could cook. There were no prices listed on the menu, that's a definite sign that the place is expensive. I picked out a sirloin steak with the usual side of a salad, baked potato and bread with a glass of sweet tea.

Tracy chose a cup of clam chowder for an appetizer and the roast duck with vegetables with a glass of water. After our order was taken, I decided to jump right out and say what had been on my mind all night.

"So, what exactly are your political views?" I asked. "I'd like to know why so many people oppose such a beautiful woman." Her smile turned to a frown. Oh boy, I thought. *I really blew it this time. Why did I have to ask?*

"I was wondering how long it would be before you asked," she said.

"Do you object to my inquiry?" I asked, "Because in the interest of a pleasant evening, I can take it back."

"Quite the contrary," she said. "I wanted to discuss this too. I'm interested in hearing your point of view as well."

"Good," I said, "ladies first." I grinned.

She smiled back. "First things first," she said. "I'm not a typical war protester. I realize that there are going to be wars. I don't blindly protest any war. I object to us being involved in a war we cannot win."

She's done her homework, I thought.

"Compare Vietnam with the other wars we've been involved in," she said. "Where is our commitment?

Where is our public support? A war cannot be won without the support of the public. What are the objectives of the United States military? These are the questions I want answers to. These are the reasons I am opposed to our involvement. Until I get answers that make sense I will keep trying." With every question and every point she made she got louder and louder. She realized this and stopped to take a deep breath. She smiled at me. "I have a tendency to get carried away sometimes."

"Has anyone ever told you how beautiful you are when you get carried away?" I asked. *Be careful, Byron,* I told myself. *You're real close to making a fool out of yourself again.* Before she could reply to the compliment, the waiter appeared with our food. I let the comment drop.

We made small talk during dinner. The food was delicious as I expected. After we finished our dinner, the waiter asked if we wanted dessert. We both declined and just ordered a cup of coffee. After the table was cleared and our coffee poured, Tracy leaned across the table.

"I'm still waiting for your comments," she said.

I thought for a minute then said, "My views as a private citizen mirror yours. I feel exactly as you do and I wish more people in Washington shared our ideas. But you must understand that I'm not a private citizen." I think my tone began to rise. "I am an officer in the United States Army, duly sworn to do a job. I will do my job to the best of my ability even if it means to kill or be killed. And I'm not sure it would be considered a plus to my character but I'm damn good at what I do."

"Well said, Captain Allison," Tracy said, smiling.⏰⏰

I honestly could not read her by her expression and tone. I couldn't tell if she truly understood and admired what I said or if inside she was picking apart my statement and mentally trashing me and my views. She could just be humoring me, so as not to ruin the evening. Could a soldier and war protester really get along without each of them hiding a little piece of their minds from each other?

The waiter broke up what was becoming a tense silence when he came up to ask about the check. "How shall you be paying tonight, Miss?" he said, condescendingly.

"Just put it on my father's tab, Clayton McLelland."

"Very well, Ma'am," he said. "Thank you for dining with us. Have a pleasant evening."

During the drive back to her house, Tracy seemed to be in another world. And I had so much running through my head I was afraid to open my mouth because I wasn't sure what would come out. I couldn't even form a coherent statement for what I was feeling.⏹ This woman had me spellbound.

There had been an awful lot of awkward silences in the few hours since I first met Tracy. She was a difficult person to read, that is, if it actually is possible to pick up on signals from any woman.

Tracy broke the silence first. "When do you leave for Washington?" she asked.

"I have a flight out the day after tomorrow" I said. Though my mind was screaming. *Never! I won't leave if you don't want me too.*

"The medal presentation is at 7PM the day after tomorrow," I continued. "Then there's a reception

driver to come on back if you aren't out front at that time. If I don't see you again, have a great trip to Washington DC tomorrow.
Tracy

I immediately looked at my watch. 8:30, I had plenty of time. Although I had showered last night, I wanted to shower again and check to see if I still had a pair of jeans in my bag. While I was trying to imagine what I would do at an anti-war rally the same young lady entered with my breakfast.

"I hope this is to your liking," she said, placing a plate of eggs, sausage, toast and a glass of orange juice in front of me.

"That looks fine, thank you."

"I'll be back in a few minutes to check if you need anything else," she said. Turning, she left me alone in the room. I didn't realize how hungry I was until I started eating. I was finished by the time the young lady returned.

"Can I get you anything else, perhaps a refill on your coffee?" she asked.

"No thanks," I replied, "it was all very good!" I stood and headed back upstairs. As I walked out of the dining room into a large corridor, I met Mrs. McLelland.

"Mr. Allison, I'm glad we ran into each other this morning. I didn't get a chance to speak with you last night. I was hoping we might have the opportunity to sit down and talk for a few minutes. Come, let's go into the dining room." She reached down and took my arm as we re-entered the dining room. We both took a seat and immediately the young lady appeared from out of the kitchen. After ordering us both coffee, Mrs. McLelland turned her attention back to me.

"Mr. Allison, please tell me about Clay," she said. "Is he in a great deal of danger?" I do worry about him." I could see the worry in her eyes.

"Before I get started, please call me Byron," I said.

She smiled and said, "OK Byron, and I'm Sandra."

"To answer your question truthfully, Sandra, first I need to say, what Clay is doing is dangerous." She nodded. I continued. "However, Clay is the most qualified person I know to handle the tasks before him in as efficient and safe a manner as possible." I was trying to be as diplomatic as possible, while at the same time attempting to answer her question. Diplomacy isn't one of my better qualities. We sat there in silence for a few moments before Sandra spoke again.

"I understand you and Tracy had dinner together last night."

"Yes, ma'am we did," I said. "Tracy is a very interesting person."

Sandra smiled and said, "Interesting is an understatement. Tracy gets her stubbornness from her father, I'm afraid. Tracy is the polar opposite from Clayton in some ways, but on the other hand, she's Clayton made over."

I smiled at the thought of the comparison. "I'm meeting her later this morning to attend a rally," I added.

Sandra's eyes suddenly grew large as she looked at me. "Oh, my word," she exclaimed. "Why would Tracy invite you to one of her protest rallies?"

I gave a short laugh before replying. "Tracy and I discussed each other's viewpoints on a number of things. I believe this is her way of allowing me to see things from her perspective. To be honest, I'm looking forward to it," I said with a smile. What I didn't say was I wasn't necessarily looking forward to the rally as much as I was looking forward to the opportunity of spending time with Tracy. I got the feeling Sandra saw through my words. She sat in silence for a moment before saying.

"Tracy is very dear to my heart and I wouldn't want her to be hurt."

I quickly spoke up and assured her I wouldn't let anything harm Tracy.

Sandra gave me a very curious smile and said, "Perhaps it's not the activities at the rally that concerns me."

We sat there for what seemed to me to be a very awkward minute or two before I assured her, I would never do anything to harm Tracy.

Sandra continued this uncomfortable situation by her reply. "We shall see, won't we, Mr. Allison?"
Before I could reply, Sandra stood, extended her hand and said, "I have enjoyed our little chat. I trust I haven't detained you too long, Mr. Allison."

The sudden change in her addressing me from Byron to Mr. Allison didn't go unnoticed. I quickly stood to face her. Holding her hand, I said, "Mrs. McLelland, I wouldn't do anything to cause you, Mr. McClelland and especially Tracy any problems in any manner."

Sandra squeezed my hand softly before saying "You're a good man Mr. Allison, I look forward to seeing you again soon. You are welcome in our home anytime." Releasing my hand, she turned and walked out of the room.

I remained standing there alone in the room trying to figure out just what Sandra was telling me. Realizing the time, I headed back to my room to get ready to meet Tracy.

Chapter 7 - Protest

I walked out the front door at 10:55 just as the car pulled up. The driver stepped out of the driver's side and said, "Mr. Allison, I presume?" I nodded as he opened the back door of the Lincoln Town car. I climbed in still trying to get my mind around the conversation with Sandra. The ride to the rally location was uneventful. As I exited the car the driver spoke for the first time since leaving the house.

"Mr. Allison, you need to be very careful. "These are advertised as peaceful rallies, but they're some here that try to cause problems."

I thanked the driver for his advice. I admitted to myself, his warning made the hair on my neck stand up. I turned and saw a crowd of around 50 or 60 people gathered around a small podium. On the stage was some guy with a bullhorn shouting some words about stopping the war. I wasn't really paying him any attention. My focus was on finding Tracy. I spotted her as she came from behind the stage. Her beauty was radiant. She had a glow on her face like nothing I've ever seen. She saw me and came running. Before I could say a word, she threw her arms around my neck and kissed me. I was caught totally off guard and it must have shown. After the kiss she stepped back, looked at me and said, "Let me guess, you've never had a woman kiss you before," she chuckled. I wanted to reply but she gave me no chance. Taking my hand, she led me into the crowd.

Just before we entered this large mass of humanity, she stopped and whispered in my ear, "You look great in the jeans and T-shirt.⯑ It's a shame your hair isn't longer," she added with a laugh.

I realized I hadn't spoken a word since getting out of the car. I was about to say how nice it was to see her. Before I could utter a word, Tracy started introducing me to some friends. Between the cheering of the crowd and the guy on stage with the bullhorn, I didn't catch most of the names of her friends. I would nod and smile and try to acknowledge the introduction.

Finally, the dude with the bullhorn quit shouting. As he finished his rhetoric, the crowd calmed down somewhat. Tracy then informed me, the group was about to march over to a war monument and join some others who were protesting. I immediately drew back at the thought of going to a war monument with a protesting group.

Tracy must have sensed my reaction. She reached up and gave me a peck on the cheek and whispered, "It will be ok; a few people will speak. I don't expect you to agree with them, but it's just the price you will have to pay for the privilege of taking me to lunch afterwards." She smiled, and took me by the hand.

The whole group of people started moving like a school of fish. No one breaking ranks, just a mass of humanity moving together. It wasn't a long walk before we arrived at a WWII monument. A woman was shouting to the crowd something about how all wars are unnecessary. She continued to claim all wars are just to help the rich get richer. I found it ironic, she was standing in front of a monument, honoring the very people that died to give her the right to protest.

After the woman finished spouting out her words of bullshit a guy walked up to the monument with a flag in his right hand and a propane torch in his left. I felt Tracy trying to grab my arm as I started moving. I quickly shoved a few people out of my way as I approached the guy with the flag. He was trying to light the propane torch as I got closer. In a forceful voice I told him, he wasn't going to burn that flag.

My reaction caught him off guard as he looked around and said, "I'm going to burn this flag and there's not a damn thing you can do."

I reached out to grab the flag from his hand just as he swung the still unlit propane torch at my head. The torch missed my head and deflected off my shoulder. Without hesitation, I came around and hit him in the jaw with my left hand. He went down but not before I grabbed the flag. I turned just as another guy charged me from the crowd. I had time to brace myself for his onslaught and was able to grab his arm, as I twisted and threw him to the ground. He hit the grass screaming as I wrenched his arm until it went limp. He was still screaming as I released his limp arm. It was then I was knocked to the ground myself, falling onto the still screaming dude. I rolled and immediately came to my feet as this third guy tried to throw a punch at my face. Moving quickly to my left, I kicked, striking the guy in the groin. The military teaches a soldier to never fight fair. Being fair can get you killed. With the third assailant now on the ground, I quickly look at the crowd when I suddenly hear someone shouting,

"Get on the ground."

I turned to see two police officers; one was shouting and the other was standing with his gun drawn. I slowly raised my hands, still holding the flag, and tried to explain I wasn't a threat. The crowd started to disperse, as the officer with the gun came closer. The second officer kept shouting for me to get on the ground, face down. Reluctantly, I complied. Once on the ground, the officer proceeded to handcuff me. Once he had me restrained, the other officer holstered his firearm. Together, they lifted me to my feet. I started to protest their actions but realized it would be fruitless. Standing there I saw the flag laying on the ground at my feet. I squatted down and with my now cuffed hand, I picked up the flag. One of the officers instructed me to drop the flag.

I looked at both of them and said, "You might want to pull that firearm back out and use it now? I'm a Captain in the United States Army, and I'll die before I drop this flag."

They both looked at one another for a moment. One of the officers took me by the arm and started leading me away making no attempt to take the flag from my hands. As I was being taken away, I was looking for Tracy, but never saw her. Once we got to the police car, I was placed in the back seat. The drive to the precinct was short. I was helped out of the car and escorted inside. Once inside, I was instructed to sit down on an old rusty metal chair. Still cuffed and holding the flag, I took a seat.

After about half an hour, another officer came and instructed me to follow him into a small room. He started asking me to tell him what happened. Knowing it's best to keep your mouth shut until you have an attorney present, all I said was, "My name is Byron

Allison. I'm a Captain in the US Army and I didn't start the fight."

He instructed me to stand up and follow him as he led me to a small cell. He asked me to release the flag so he could remove the cuffs. Once the cuffs were off, he handed me back the flag and motioned me to enter the cell. I did as he instructed, then he locked the cell door. I sat in the cell thinking what a mess I have made of things. I've lost any hope with Tracy, I'm in jail. I don't know anyone to call and I really don't want to get the Army involved. I sat there for a couple of hours trying to figure out my options. It was obvious to me, I wouldn't be making my flight to Washington tomorrow, and would probably never see Tracy again.

I heard footsteps as a different officer approached the cell door. He unlocked the door and asked me to follow him. We walked down one hall through a couple of doors, past a few small rooms before coming to our destination. The officer opened the door and instructed me to enter. As I entered, I knew I must really be in a pile of shit. At one end of a large table sat Clayton McLelland and some other guy in a real expensive suit. They were talking with what I later learned was the Chief of Police, whose name was Dan, something. Clayton wasn't really shouting, but he was talking in a rather forceful tone as he addressed the Chief:

"Dan, do you have any idea what your people have done? This man is a war hero, he's enroute to Washington D.C to talk with the President and to receive the Congressional Medal of Honor. Do you have any idea what the press will do with this? After my Public Relation people get a hold of it, it will be as

60

though you arrested Mother Teresa. I can assure you; it will be the end of your career."

Clayton was talking as though I wasn't even in the room. No one had acknowledged my presence. Clayton went on with what could be described as my defense.

"Damn it, Dan, you can't afford to charge this man; again, it would be the death drop for you. Elections are only 6 months away. I suggest you refrain from any charges. "No record of this." You can issue a statement that your officers brought Byron here for his protection. That will cover you and your officers." There was a couple of minutes of silence before the Chief of Police spoke. "Clayton, this man is responsible for breaking one man's arm, kicking another in the balls and very possibly breaking the jaw of the third."

For the first time, Clayton looked at me and smiled before turning his attention back to the Chief, "Dan, as I understand it, Byron was defending himself. I can produce witnesses that will testify one of these guys swung at Byron. I'm telling you Dan, this isn't a battle you want to fight. You know Hamilton." Clayton motioned to the guy in the expensive suit. "He's our attorney. We plan to leave here with Byron either on bail or as a free man. I've already spoken to Judge Harrison and he's agreed to set bail. All I need to do is call him."

The Chief sat there and rubbed his forehead before speaking. He looked up at me, still standing there, holding the flag. "Mr. Allison," he said. "I'm going to let you go, there won't be any official record of this event. "You are free to go."

Clayton almost jumped out of his chair saying, "Great, Dan, you won't regret this." Then he turned to the attorney and said, "Damn, I love it when a plan comes together."

Before I could say thanks, the Chief stood up and left the room. Clayton went out the door and the attorney motioned for me to follow Clayton. As we passed the main desk, I saw one of the officers that arrested me. I turned to give them a piece of my mind when Hamilton laid his hand on my shoulder and said, "We're done here, just let it drop."

I turned and walked out the door.

There was a car waiting outside the precinct. I found it somewhat ironic, the car was sitting in a 'No Parking' zone in front of a police station. After we got seated in the car, Clayton turned and said, "Byron, the driver is going to drop Hamilton and me off at the office. Afterwards, he will take you to the house. I suspect Tracy will be there waiting."

The thought of Tracy being at the house excited and worried me at the same time. I looked first at Hamilton before turning my attention to Clayton.

"Mr. McLelland, I want first to thank you for helping me and second I want to apologize for causing a situation that required your help." Clayton laughed out loud before speaking.

"Byron, you owe me no apology and I am more than glad to be able to help. Hell, I would have expected no less from you for stopping that asshole from burning the flag."

That was when I realized I was still holding the flag. Clayton went on to say, "If you have no plans for the flag, I would like to have it for my trophy room. After all, there's a hell of a story behind it. Again, you do not owe me an apology. However, I would love to be a fly on the wall when you talk with Tracy."

I handed Clayton the flag. This time it was Hamilton that broke out in laughter. Clayton continued, "I believed I warned you, Tracy can be, well how can I put this? Never mind, you are about to find out for yourself."

This time he and Hamilton both laughed. The remaining ride to their office was in silence. As Hamilton exited the car, he looked at me and said; "Good luck Mr. Allison, you are going to need all the luck you can get." He and Clayton both were laughing as they walked away.

Chapter 8 - Fall in Love

By now it was starting to get dark. Suddenly I realized how tired I was. I've gone days without sleep back in Nam and now I was worn out from just one day's activity. The ride to the house took the best part of an hour, but it seemed like only a few minutes. The car pulled up to the house.

I continued to sit there and I suspect the driver noticed me not moving, turned and asked, "Is there something else you need, Mr. Allison?"

I smiled and said, "No thanks," as I slid out of the car. I walked up the steps. Before I could reach for the door it opened.

The same young lady from this morning smiled and said, "Welcome back Mr. Allison. Ms. Tracy asked if you would join her in the living room."

I thanked her and headed down the hall. The double doors were standing open as I approached. I entered. Sitting in a chair was Tracy. First thing I noticed was the fact that Tracy wasn't smiling. I didn't wait for her to speak. I walked over and sat down in the chair next to her.

After a moment of silence, I spoke, "Tracy, I want to apologize, not for what I did. There's no way I could stand by and allow anyone to burn our flag. I don't regret my actions in that respect. However, I do regret allowing myself to be in that position and causing you any grief. In retrospect, me agreeing to attend the rally was a mistake. I was just excited at the chance to spend time with you and I didn't properly think the situation through. I'll be leaving in the morning. It's probably best for everyone. I know I have embarrassed you, perhaps your mother as well and caused your dad a lot of trouble. Speaking of your dad, I want to thank you for calling him. I'm not sure how I would have handled the situation without his help."

Up to this point, Tracy hadn't uttered a word. I stood and turned to face her. "Tracy, I'm really sorry it all turned out this way. Good night."

As I started to turn, she spoke up. "You still owe me lunch."

I understood what she said, but it still didn't register. I looked back at her and realized she was smiling. She said again, "You offered me lunch earlier today. I still want lunch."

A smile came across my face as I asked, "Where do you want to go? I am ready."

She stood and said, "I've asked Darlene to prepare us something. She has it ready in the private dining room."

Tracy reached out, taking my hand as we walked out of the living room. We walked into a small but very elegant dining room capable of seating six people. Tracy took a seat and I took the chair next to her.

Darlene entered from a side door and asked, "Ms. Tracy, I've prepared grilled chicken sandwiches with potato salad and coleslaw, I hope that is adequate." Tracy chuckled, "Darlene, you know that is my favorite. It will be fine, thank you."

It wasn't but a couple of minutes later before our food was sitting on the table. Once Darlene was out of the room, Tracy spoke; "Before we start to eat, there's something I want to say."

I thought to myself, OK here it comes. I turned slightly to face Tracy, bracing myself for what was to come. Tracy continued, "I'm not happy with today's events. Perhaps not for the reasons you might think. The flag burning episode wasn't supposed to happen. Before inviting you, I checked the agenda. I wouldn't have invited you if I had known." She hesitated for a moment before continuing; "What you did to those three guys I wish could have been prevented. Given the circumstances, I understand. To be truthful, I'm glad you stopped the flag from being burned. Even I draw a line at that. From a personal perspective, you really kicked ass." She flashed me her soft sexy smile as she said, "Let's eat, I'm hungry." I realized I hadn't eaten since breakfast and she didn't have to say that twice. We ate in silence, each caught up in our own thoughts.

Once finished Tracy spoke up, "Byron, again I'm sorry I put you in that situation. I hope you will forgive me."

I reached and took a sip of my tea, before replying, "You have no reason to apologize, and there's nothing to forgive you over. As far as I'm concerned, today never happened."

She smiled and we sat again in silence for a few seconds. Then she reached and took me by the hand before saying, "It's going to be hard to forget today happened. I will always remember how you handled the three guys that attacked you. You were fantastic." She squeezed my hand before continuing, "I know you must be tired, I certainly am. Byron Allison, I know you are leaving in the morning, but I hope you will see fit to return soon. I owe you, at the least, a dinner for what I put you through today." She reached over and gave me a kiss on the cheek before getting up and leaving the room. I tried to get my thoughts together before getting up and heading to my room.

I walked into my room and, not bothering to turn on the light, stripped and turned on the shower in the bathroom. I stepped in, the hot water running down my back reminding me how tired I was. And how glad I was to be home, well, close to home anyway. In Nam, a cold shower was considered a luxury and a hot shower was unheard of.

I could've stayed in the shower until I had used up all the hot water in the country, but I knew I needed to get some sleep. I stepped out of the shower and dried myself off. I exited the bathroom into the still dark room. I pulled the sheets back and fell into the bed. Tired as I was, sleep was the farthest thing from my mind. I laid there, trying to sort out the events of the day.

Suddenly almost instinctively, the hairs on the back of my neck stood straight up. I got a cold chill down my spine. I realized that I wasn't alone in the room! I opened my eyes and saw the silhouette of a person leaning over my bed. I could smell a sweet familiar perfume.

"Tracy," I said.

She climbed into the bed with me. "Shut up and kiss me before I change my mind."

I woke early the next morning and she was gone. I lay there a minute or two before I realized that it was not a dream. I dressed, and went downstairs. The housekeeper met me at the stairway landing.

"Mr. Allison, good morning," she said.

"Thank you," I replied. "Is Tracy up yet? I wanted to tell her goodbye."

"Ms. Tracy has already left for the day, but she asked if I would give you this," said the housekeeper as she handed me an envelope.

I tucked the envelope in my jacket pocket and headed outside. I was anxious to read the letter, but at the same time I was afraid of what it might say.

After I got settled in the car and was out of sight of the McLelland house, I pulled the envelope from my pocket and opened it. The handwritten letter inside read:

Dear Byron

> *I hope you don't think badly of me after*
> *Last night. I don't know what came over me,*
> *But I have no regrets. I truly want to see*
> *You again.*
>
> > *Love,*
> > *Tracy.*

During my flight to Washington, Tracy was all I could think about.

Chapter 9 - The Meeting

When the alarm went off, I rolled over and almost knocked it across the room. I lay there for a moment thinking of Tracy, remembering how I felt that night. I could almost smell the remnants of her perfume.

As I lay there in a lumpy bed in a cheap hotel room in New Orleans, I gave thoughts to the chain of events that put me there and changed my life. How could one event have an effect on so many others? This was not the first time that I had these thoughts. I have wondered a million times what we would be doing now if only Tracy had...

Ring, ring. The phone abruptly interrupted my thoughts. I realized that fifteen minutes had gone by. I must have dozed off.

Ring, ring. I grabbed the receiver and attempted to say hello without sounding like I had been asleep, but instead, I practically shouted into the phone.

"Well, aren't we grouchy before we have our morning coffee?" It was Clay. "It's 7:45, bro. And we have an 8:00 appointment with fate."

"Get me a large cup of black coffee to go and I will meet you in the lobby," I said. I slammed down the receiver. Man, I really felt bad.

I dragged myself out of bed and to the bathroom. *Get yourself together, Byron.* I told myself. *You are supposed to be a leader of men.*

I chuckled out loud when I realized what I must look like standing there in my skivvies in a dimly lit room of a sleazy hotel. Certainly not the picturesque scene meant to instill confidence in other men.

Having showered the night before, I washed my face, brushed my teeth, combed my hair and got dressed in a matter of minutes. I was on the elevator by 7:53.

When I stepped off the elevator in the lobby, Clay was standing there with a large Styrofoam cup of coffee.

"I come with a peace offering," he said as he thrust the cup into my hand. He was a real wise ass sometimes. We headed towards the front doors.

"I hope you feel better than you look," Clay said.

"Shut up and let me drink my coffee," I said.

"Sir! Sir!" I heard a voice calling behind me. I turned around and saw Tony Danley running towards me.

"Sir, I believe you dropped this," he said.

I extended my hand and in it he placed a four-leaf clover. Tony winked. I nodded at him and he walked away. It wasn't hard to figure out that was Tony's way of saying good luck. Clay and I exited the hotel.

There was a blue Ford sedan waiting outside. The two men in the front seat, I recognized from Birmingham. Clay and I got in the back. As the car pulled away from the curb, I looked at my watch. It was 8:01.

The car pulled up in front of a building in the old warehouse section of New Orleans. After two short blasts of the horn, the roll-up doors started moving. The driver pulled inside and the door rolled back down behind us. We were on the other side of town from where we started and I realized that not a single word had been spoken during the trip. I stepped out of the car and it took my eyes a few seconds to adjust to the sparsely lit warehouse. I could tell by the smell of

69

diesel and gasoline fumes that this warehouse had recently been used.⊠ The floor was littered with small pieces of paper and hundreds of cigarette butts.

The driver uttered the first words spoken since we left the hotel. "Both of you, follow me."

I hadn't heard this guy speak since he and his buddy escorted me to the plane in Birmingham two days earlier.

Clay and I did as we were told and followed the driver. Our other escort stayed behind. We walked across the warehouse into a corridor. Halfway down the hall our escort stopped, pointed to a steel door and said, "In there. The Colonel is waiting."

Clay looked at me. I shrugged my shoulders and motioned towards the door. He turned the knob, put his shoulder against the door and pushed it open. He stepped back and bowed.

"After you, oh great leader," he said, flashing me his ever-present shitty smile.

"I'm trying real hard to like you but you are not making it easy," I replied as I stepped across the threshold.

"I can see neither of you have lost your sense of humor," said a voice from inside the room. My eyes had to adjust again to the lighting. Clay shut the door behind us with a heavy thud.

The Colonel came towards us to shake our hands.

"Byron, how are you doing?" he said. "And Clay it's good to see you. How is your dad doing?"

The Colonel has a habit of asking a question and not waiting on an answer before continuing. There are two reasons why he would do this. One is because he already knows the answer and the other is because, like a barrage of artillery fire, a barrage of questions will keep an opponent off guard and on the defensive.

"Byron, have a seat," the Colonel said, motioning to a chair. I don't believe he had taken a breath since we walked in the room.

"I have something I want Clay to do before we get started. We'll be right back. Fix yourself a cup of coffee," he motioned toward the coffee pot. "You look like you could use some."

Clay and the Colonel exited the room. I fixed a cup of coffee and sat down.

Sitting there, waiting for the Colonel and Clay to return, my thoughts drifted back to that night with Tracy and the events that followed.

Chapter 10 - Standing up the President

The morning after my night with Tracy, I had left California and flown by military jet to Washington, D.C. In D.C, I was met by a military driver and taken to a hotel. A nice hotel. *Better than the one I woke up in this morning.* I spent a night in the hotel. I was scheduled to have a late lunch the next day with Senator Joseph Dial of California and several of his cronies before the ceremony. It was at lunch that I received life-changing news.

We were sitting in the Senate dining room when a man I couldn't quite place came in. He seemed familiar; a short, fat, happy looking fellow. I had seen him before. He walked over to Senator Dial and spoke to him and then turned to me.

"Hello Captain. We meet again so soon," he said. I must have looked puzzled, he laughed and extended his hand.

"My name is Albert French. Senator from Alabama. We met two days ago at a reception in your honor at Clayton McLelland's house."

"I'm sorry Senator," I said. "These last couple of days have been rather hectic."

"No need to apologize, Captain, I understand," he replied in a low, strange way. Like he knew something that I didn't, but should.

Senator French turned and started talking to the man seated beside me and before I could collect my thoughts Senator Dial came over to me with a group of people and started introducing me. I rose from my chair so I could shake hands and act remotely interested. My back was to Senator French but I could hear him talking. I swear I heard Tracy's name and the word *'accident.'* I spun around, nearly knocking my chair over. I grabbed Senator French by the shoulder maybe a little harder than I should have...

"Did you just say something about Tracy being in an accident?" I asked, trying not to sound like I was in a panic.

"You mean you haven't heard?" asked the Senator.

"Heard what?" I asked maybe a little louder than I should have.

Senator French's face turned ghostly white and the whole room was watching me.

"I'm sorry to be the one to have to tell you this but Tracy was in a car accident this morning."

"How is she?" I asked, managing to lower my voice.⁊ I knew the answer before he even said anything. The expression on his face spoke more than words could.⯑ I have seen that expression before. Hell, I've had that same expression before when I had to write a soldier's mother and say that her little boy was coming home in a body bag.

Senator French cleared his throat.

"Tracy was returning from a demonstration when a car traveling on the wrong side of the road plowed head on into her car. She was pronounced dead at the scene."⯑ His voice almost quivered with those words.

"The driver of the other car," he continued, "was drunk and sustained only minor injuries."

From there the Senator broke out into a speech about changing the laws and dealing with DUI offenders but I was no longer listening.

I bolted out the door of the dining hall into the hallway. My driver was sitting on a bench. He jumped to his feet when he saw me.

"Soldier," I said, trying to maintain my composure. "Get the car and bring it around front. I need to go to the airport."

"Yes sir!" He snapped as he turned to leave. His stride had almost turned into a jog when Senator Dial stopped him.

"Just a minute, private!" he shouted.⯑ I hadn't even realized he was in the hallway. My driver halted.

"The captain will not be going anywhere just now." Turning to me, he said "Byron, the President of the United States will be presenting you with the Congressional Medal of Honor in approximately two hours. You cannot leave before then." He put his hand on my shoulder and leaned in. "Think what it would do to your career. You could be booted out of the army. You are an officer in the United States Army and the

President is your Commander-in-Chief. Nobody walks out on him." He paused and took a step back. "Come on back inside. I have some very important people still waiting to meet you." He opened the door to the dining hall and motioned for me to enter.

I stood there and looked at him for an awkward moment and then looked at my driver who I am certain had not moved since the Senator halted him.

"Soldier!" I said firmly. "My car had better be out front when I get there. I have given you an order and as long as I am a Captain in this man's army you will carry it out. Do you understand?"

"Yes sir!" he shouted and broke out into a dead run towards the exit.

I turned my attention to a very stunned Senator. In the same firm voice, I spoke very slowly, very deliberately.

"Senator, I did not ask for this luncheon nor did I ask for the medal. I am sure the President can find something else to amuse himself with today. I don't give a damn about any of this and you can all go to hell as far as I am concerned."

I turned and started very quickly down the hall towards the front doors. Behind me I could hear the Senator screaming something about a court martial and him furnishing the rope. I thought about telling the doorman to slam the door behind me for dramatic effect but thought better of it and just nodded to him as I exited. For a brief second before he closed the door, I could hear what sounded like an angry mob following me. My car pulled up just as I had reached the bottom step.

I opened the door and slid into the backseat. The hair on the back of my neck stood up when I realized that the young private was not the driver of my car. In his place was a rusty-looking Master Sergeant with an MP band around his right shoulder.

"You people act fast," I said. "I didn't expect the MP's so soon."

"Just doing my job, sir," he said.

I looked out of the window in time to see Senator Dial bursting out the door followed by Mr. French, several other senators and four MP Sergeants. I looked back at my new driver and leaned towards the front seat.

"From one combat veteran to another, I need your help and I need it now. I don't have time to explain it but you would be doing me a big favor if we could just leave."

Before I could say another word, and before I could promise that I would explain when there was time, the sergeant jerked the gear lever down and pulled away from the curb so fast it slung me back into my seat. I buckled my seat belt.

"The airport please," I said.

"Captain, I don't know what you did to stir up those panty waist politicians," he said. "And I don't even want to know, but it's safe to say that you have succeeded in getting me into some deep shit."

"I know Sergeant," I said halfway apologetically. "I really do appreciate what you did."

"No problem," he said. "Anyone who has earned the Congressional Medal of Honor has earned my help anytime. Besides, I miss the adventure of being in combat. This is the most excitement I've had in years."

"Glad I could help you," I said.

He genuinely seemed like a nice guy.

"Do you know the fastest way to the airport?"

"Yes, Sir I do," he said. He glanced at me in the rear-view mirror.

"Sir, it's not really any of my business but..." he trailed off.

"Go ahead, sergeant," I said. "At this point it really is your business."

"Yes, sir I guess it is," he agreed. "Sir, I don't think it's a good idea for you to go to the airport expecting to jump a flight. Not in your dress blues. By now, every MP in town is looking for an infantry captain in dress uniform."

"Thank you, sergeant. That's twice you've saved my ass. Drop me off at the Hyatt Regency." How many times has an officer been saved, one way or another, by the wisdom and experience of a good NCO, I thought.

The remainder of the drive to the hotel was done in silence. The sergeant pulled the car up to the curb. I leaned up over the front seat and extended my hand.

"Sergeant," I said as he shook my hand. "Maybe the day will come when I can be of service to you. Hopefully in not as drastic a situation. I'm indebted to you and I don't even know your name."

"Master Sergeant Anthony Danley, sir," he said "And don't you worry about me. My thirty years are up in two weeks. I am hanging it up then and there's not much the army can do to me between now and then." His face took a more serious look. "Got a son in Nam. He's a leg like you and me. Name's Tony. Who knows, you might be able to do him a favor someday." I nodded.

76

"Better get going sir," he said. "Won't be long before they show up here. You take care and watch your backside"

"Thanks again Sergeant Danley," I said as I got out of the car.

"Glad to do it, Captain," he said. I shut the door and saluted him. I saw him raise his right hand to his brow as he drove off.

I sprinted to my room and changed into civilian clothes. I crammed my military clothes into my suitcase. It had been thirty minutes since I left the Senate. In ninety minutes, I would become the first army captain in history to stand up the President of the United States.

Chapter 11 - Escaping

The reality of it all was starting to settle in. Career-wise I was dead. The chance of me getting out of the hotel was slim at best and the chances of me actually making it to the airport were nil. Boarding an airplane? I had a better chance of making a snowman in hell. I don't even have money for a ticket. But I had to get to California. I just had to. But why? I couldn't have fallen in love with Tracy in such a short amount of time. Or could I?

The phone rang and I jumped. I started not to answer it but I figured why not? I'm dead anyway.

"Hello? Captain Allison?"

"Who wants to know?" I said.

"Captain this is Joseph Dial. No time to explain, listen carefully. There will be a car and driver waiting to pick you up in front of your hotel..."

"Is this some kind of trick?" I interrupted.

"Captain, I haven't the time nor the inclination to play games with you," he said, sounding rather irritated. "The driver will take you to a private hangar where a corporate jet is waiting. I will explain on the way."

"On the way where," I asked, expecting to be told I'm going to my own flogging.

"California."

I nearly dropped the telephone.

"Captain, are you there?" Dial said.

"I'm still here."

"Good. Will I see you at the airport?"

"Yes sir," Dial hung up the phone. I stood there listening to the dial tone for a moment before hanging up the phone. I knew there was a God in Nam, he'd seen me through too many times. Now I was beginning to believe there was a God here too.

I finished getting my bags together. I threw some necessities in my overnight bag. I left a note on my large suitcase requesting that it be delivered to the BOQ (Bachelor Officer Quarters) at Fort Belvoir, Virginia. I laid a twenty-dollar bill on the suitcase and hoped that my maid was an honest person. I grabbed my overnight bag and headed out, knowing that anyone looking for me would be waiting by the lobby elevators. I avoided the elevators completely. I took the fire escape stairs. They came out into a back corner of the lobby. I eased the door open and looked around. The lobby was busy with people coming and going. My heart stopped briefly when I saw two MP's arguing with the desk clerk.

"Damn it boy," the MP yelled. "I don't want you to ring his room and announce us. I want his room number and I want it now!"

It was a straight shot to the front door and the front desk was on the other side of the lobby from me, however it was a very small lobby. There wasn't much more than a couch, a couple of end tables and a fake fichus tree separating us. But as long as they didn't turn around, I could make it. The clerk saw me and our eyes locked for a moment. Then he looked back at the MPs. I took my chance and started walking.

"I'm sorry sir," he said. "It is hotel policy not to give out room numbers. I don't even think Captain Allison is here. However, if you promise not to tell how you got it, I'll look up his room number for you." I caught his eye again as I cleared the other side of the MPs and my hand was on the door. There was a faint smile on his lips. He fumbled through some papers.

"Quit drag-assing around and give me the number!" The sergeant bellowed.

"Here it is, Captain Allison is in room number..."

I was already out the door. If only that kid knew how much I was indebted to him. I was racking up all kinds of debts today.

"Are you Captain Allison?" I was startled by this man that appeared out of nowhere. I took a deep breath and nodded. This was the moment of truth. The man raised his hand. I expected to be jumped. Instead, a limousine pulled up to the curb. We got in and took off. By now I figured the MPs were in my room. Maybe they would see to it that my bag got to the BOQ in Fort Belvoir. I couldn't help but chuckle.

The trip to the hanger took twenty minutes. There was an eight-passenger Lear jet sitting on the runway, engines already going. The driver pulled right up to it.

"Sir, you must hurry," he said. "They are waiting."

"Thank you." I exited the car.

An attendant grabbed my bag from my hand and escorted me onto the plane. Senator Dial was already on the plane. I had barely gotten through the door when we started taxiing down the runway. I grabbed a seat across the table from Dial.

Once we were safely in the air, the senator got up and poured us a couple of drinks. He handed me one, sat down and said,

"Captain you sure as hell have a way of making high level enemies. I apologize for Senator French being the one to break the news about Tracy, especially in the manner in which he did. He just assumed you had heard. I know you and Clay were military acquaintances but I never realized you and Tracy were, well, I didn't know you were so close. After I saw your reaction, I called Clayton. He asked that I get you to California as quickly as possible." He paused for a moment, gulped down about half his drink and continued.

"Tracy was returning home from one of those rallies she was so famous for. Another car that was being driven by," he paused and pulled a small piece of paper out of his shirt pocket. He continued, "driven by a Mr. William Crawford." He flicked the piece of paper down on the table. "Seems Mr. Crawford had been drinking. He was coming down that two lane stretch of coastal highway when his car crossed the center line and collided with Tracy's head on." Dial stopped to finish his drink. "She was killed instantly. Crawford was treated for cuts and bruises and was released from the hospital and promptly arrested for DUI and vehicular homicide. His parents were waiting to bail him out but I don't think they are going to be able to buy him out of this one. Not this time."

Dial got up and poured himself another drink. I tried to relax. I realized I had been sitting tense and stone-faced since the plane took off. I hadn't even sipped my drink. I took a couple of quick sips and a deep breath.

"What do you mean by *'this time'*?" I asked.

Dial thought for a minute before speaking.

"Crawford had a history of drinking and driving. He's been arrested nine times for driving under the influence. His family has strong local ties and plenty of money. His uncle is a judge. All that has managed to keep him out of jail. About two years ago he was involved in a hit and run accident. A twelve-year-old boy on a bicycle was badly injured. He was unconscious for nearly a week. When he finally woke up, he described Crawford's car and identified Crawford himself. He was the paper boy on Crawford's Street so he easily recognized Crawford and his car. He was arrested based on this. Rumor has it that the Crawford family paid the boy's hospital bills and gave the family $100,000 to drop the charges." Senator Dial returned to his seat. We sat in silence for a moment.

"I spoke with Clayton briefly. He's holding up well but I don't know for how long. Mrs. McLelland is sedated. Clayton and the family physician thought it in her best interest for now that she rests while others handled the arrangements. I pulled some strings to get Clay home from Nam. And my staff is currently working on your problem. The Honorable Senator French will recover quickly. The President is another story. He'll want your ass on a silver platter and your scalp to fly from the White House flag pole. Fortunately, you have two things in your favor. You are still a recipient of the Congressional Medal of Honor, ceremony or not, you still have that honor. And Washington quickly forgets. Not necessarily forgives...but forgets."

I was so tired. Dial seemed to read my mind.

"It's been a long day. There are some bunks in the back of the plane. Go crawl in one and get some sleep. You've got a few hours before we get to California."

Chapter 12 - Briefings and Gearing Up

The squeak of the heavy metal door brought me out of my semi trance.

"Byron, it's good to be working together again," said Colonel Mathews. He closed the door. "I'm going to brief you on this mission and then you and Clay can get together with the intelligence reports. After you've had a chance to look that over, we'll address any final questions you may have."

The Colonel sat down at his desk, opened a drawer and pulled out two large manila envelopes. He laid one to the side and opened the other.

"Byron, I'm going to skip the formal jargon about our activities not being part of the U.S. government. You've heard all that before. It is safe to say that there are elements of Washington anxiously awaiting the information we hope you will bring back. With that said, we have reports coming out of Central America of a major military build-up. It appears to be in this area here." He slid a map towards me and pointed to a circled area. He then pulled from the envelope some satellite photos and put them in front of me.

"All I see is jungle," I said.

"Precisely!" he practically shouted. "The area is all triple canopy. We cannot get pictures clear enough to make out shit from the sky. We have heat sensor images that indicate something is out there, but nothing concrete. All we want from you and your people is to go in, look around, take some pictures and get out. Two days in, one day recon, two days out. Nice, neat and nobody knows anything." He leaned back in his chair. Something about the expression on his face made me uneasy.

"Colonel," I said, looking back and forth between the pictures in front of me. "Do you really think it will be that easy?"

"No, I don't," he said matter-of-factly. "That's the very reason I sent for you and why I put together this special team. If I was as convinced as the boys on the hill, I could have sent someone else."

"But why would anyone want to build-up an army in such a remote area? How are supplies getting in and, why does anybody here give a damn?"

Colonel Mathews sat there for a moment before responding. "The *Why* of the matter is open for speculation. A few hundred miles to the east is the Panama Canal. That's one thought. The whole area is a political hotbed based on the rumors. A well-equipped force could overthrow any two governments simultaneously. Our country would lose major industrial interest if something like that was to happen. Besides, the boys on the hill always get nervous when any country starts building up military force. Now I hope that answers two of your questions. But how the supplies are getting in is what I want *you* to answer. Your team is being brought in as we speak; they will be outfitted in the basics: camos, radios, c-rations, et cetera. After you and Clay finish with the intelligence reports you can decide on weapons, ammo and such. Turn your weapon request and ammo load to my assistant. He will see to everything you need. Tonight, all of you will board a seaplane and fly to this island here." The Colonel slid aside the satellite photographs and pointed to a tiny speck in the map. "There you will meet your extraction group and co-ordinate your radio frequencies. Then you will draw weapons and proceed by boat across to this area," he slid his finger from the speck on the map through the ocean to another speck on the map. "It's about twenty-five miles. The boats are specially equipped to get you within ten feet of the beach. The team will leave the island just after dark tomorrow night. You will then travel to here before daylight," he placed his finger on the shore of the mainland. This is a fairly open area and requires night travel. Once you reach the jungle it's your call from there."

"Byron," his voice lowered and his face turned serious, "I have seen the reports. Don't kid yourself. There is something out there. Exactly what, why or how many we don't know. Hopefully it's just a military maniac and a small group of weekend warriors that want to play war. The terrain will not allow much in the way of support if you get into trouble, so be careful. If it looks like things are going to get hot, get out.⊠ Remember this is a recon, not D-Day." He stood up from his chair.

"I'll get Clay back in here. You've got work to do." He exited the room.

I stood up and stretched. I walked to the coffee pot and poured Clay and myself a cup. I could feel the adrenaline starting to flow.

84

Clay came in and we went back over the intelligence reports. I told him everything the Colonel had told me. I instructed Clay to brief the team on everything but the exact locations. I wanted to wait until we were underway. Plus, I wanted to talk to our extraction group. Chances are they are the ones providing the intelligence reports. I wanted as much information as possible before we went in. I wanted to be able to tell each man what he was going up against. I never believed in lying or withholding information when a man's life is at stake.

Later that evening the team got together. We drank coffee, ate c-rations and told stories. Clay was going over the maps for the hundredth time. Looking over this group I knew, as everyone else present knew; this was the best outfit of fighting men in the world. At least we thought so. And that was all that mattered.

I stood and loudly cleared my throat. Clay laid the maps down and a hush filled the room.

"Gentlemen," I said. "Before we proceed beyond this building, I have a couple of questions. Based on what you have been told so far, does anyone have any questions? Does anyone have any reservations or doubt about what is expected of you?" No one made a sound. I continued.

"Is there anyone who wants to drop out for any reason? If so, no one will question your reason nor think any less of you. Now is the time for that kind of decision. Once we leave here you are committed and expected to do exactly as instructed. This team depends on everyone giving one hundred and fifty percent."

Before I could say another word, someone farted. A loud, explosive, lengthy fart. The room erupted in laughter. Tony Danley jumped to his feet, "Damn Andrews!" he yelled "What are you trying to do? Shit in your pants?"

"What are you talking about, white boy," bellowed Andrews. "I didn't fart!"

"The hell you didn't!" continued Tony. "I can smell a black fart from a white fart any day!"

Realizing I was still standing and not likely done with my speech. Tony took his seat. The laughter, backslapping and cussing subsided.

"Alright," I said. "I take it we are all going on a vacation together. I hope that's what it turns out to be. Everyone meets in the main warehouse in fifteen minutes."

I turned to leave the room but not before the horrid smell had found its way to my nose.

Once in the main warehouse we turned in all our personal belongings and identification. We were issued watches, cigarettes and lighters, and compasses, all in unlabeled packs. Each man was also issued a P-38 can opener, a 3-day supply of rations and a K-Bar knife and sheath with sharpening stone. One by one, each man examined the sharpness of his knife and made a mental note to work on the edge. Everyone was issued a M-16-A2, 10 clips each having a 20-round capacity. In addition to their rifle, each one was issued a 9MM Beretta side arm. I watched as everyone put their newly acquired belongings in a rut sack.

Once everyone was ready, we boarded the truck for the short trip to the dock. Climbing out of the truck at the dock, the first thing I noticed was the paint of the seaplane. It was a military plane that had been converted to handle cargo. That was obvious by the larger cargo doors on each side. But the paint job was mismatched. A direct attempt to make the plane look old and worn out. Maybe it did from a distance, but up close you could tell this was a fairly new aircraft. In large letters down the side, it said *Gulf Caribbean Air Cargo*. I didn't have to wonder who owned the plane.

The harder the CIA tried to hide, the more obvious their presence was.

Within minutes we were aboard and airborne. The flight was going to take about four hours. The engines made so much noise that talking was impossible. Communication was limited to shouting and hand gestures which did not make for good communication. So, each man slipped into his own little mental world. Several were going through the slow sliding motion of rubbing their new K-Bar across the whetstone. Some slipped into a semi-conscious sleep. Clay was studying his maps again. I picked one of them up. As I stared at it, my mind drifted back to California and Tracy.

Chapter 13 - Career Gone

A car was waiting when Senator Dial and I landed in California. We were driven to a hotel where two suites had been reserved for us. We checked in and went to our suites.

"Byron, put your bag up, settle in a bit and meet me in my suite in a few minutes," Dial said. "We have a lot to discuss."

I did as he said. When I entered his suite, he already had a drink poured for both of us. He motioned for me to sit down on the sofa.

"The first thing you need to do, Byron, is go down to the men's store located in the lobby and get yourself a couple of suits and whatever else you need. Just tell them to put it on my account. It's the least I can do considering all you have been through, besides..."

The telephone rang. Dial stopped in mid-sentence and answered it. "Hello? Yes, this is Dial." He paused. His face lit up. "Oh, hello Mathews! How's the family?" Another pause. "Yes, he's okay, all things considered. Hold on just a minute Mathews. I need to change phones." The Senator pressed the hold button on the phone and placed the receiver on the cradle. "I need to take this in the bedroom."

"I understand," I said.

Dial went into the bedroom and closed the door behind him. I resigned myself to Tracy's death. My emotions had turned from hurt and pain for Tracy to hatred for William Crawford. I wanted him to feel pain, for the pain he had caused. No, that's not what I wanted. I wanted him dead. I didn't even know the man and I wanted him dead. I am not sure how long I had been sitting there with my thoughts when Dial came out of the bedroom.

"I'm sorry Byron," he said. "We never really get away from our work."

"No need to apologize," I said.

"Now, we're clear on you getting what you need from the store. Next about your problem. In fact, that call pertained to you. I had asked a friend connected with the Pentagon to look into your situation. You know, damage control. As it turns out, things aren't as bad as they first appeared. Orders are being written assigning you, temporarily, as my military affairs advisor. That eliminates you from being AWOL. You will be getting your medal just without all the ceremonies and fanfare. It will be delivered by special courier. The president didn't want to take a chance of being stood-up-twice." Dial smiled. "Now, that's the good part. The downside of things is that the army insisted on your resignation. And in my opinion, it's your only option other than a court-martial. With Senator French and the President against you, what chance would you have? Resigning will keep your record clean and you can leave the service with dignity. Fight it and they will see to it that you lose your commission and possibly go to jail. Think about it, but don't take too long. I need to tell my people something soon."

We sat in silence for a few minutes. I mulled over my options though there wasn't much to consider.

"Tell your people to do it," I said. "Even if today had gone like it was supposed to, I would still be done as an Army Officer. As a Congressional Medal of Honor recipient, I would never be more than a recruiting poster for the army, Senator. "I looked him square in the eye. "I don't expect you to understand but I'm a combat infantry officer. A dogface, a grunt, a leg with a commission. Without the challenge of combat, I have no desire to stay in Uncle Sam's Army."

The senator smiled a devious sort of smile. He leaned in and spoke in a tone I hadn't heard until now. "Maybe, I can help you in another way. I mentioned earlier I have a friend who is connected with the Pentagon. His name is Colonel Mathews. When all is settled, I would like to introduce you to him. I think you share a mutual interest. Enough of that said for now," his tone returned to normal.

"Let's get back to more solemn matters. We are expected at the McLelland's estate at six o'clock for a wake. Family and close friends only. The funeral is tomorrow at eleven. Again, family and friends only. Go get your wardrobe in order and meet me in the lobby at 5:30."

I got up to leave, pausing at the door, I turned around and said, "Senator, I can never thank you enough for all you have done."

"Nonsense," he said. "Come back to me two years from now, look me straight in the eye and then thank me." He smiled. His tone had changed again. A cold chill went down my spine as I left the room.

As I walked down the hall, I couldn't help but feel an ominous meaning in Dial's last statement. I got on the elevator still feeling a chill down my back as the elevator door opened in the lobby. I strolled over to the men's store. As I entered, I was greeted by an elderly man.

"May I help you sir," he said.

"I need two dark blue suits along with two white shirts and ties," I said.

"What type of tie would you prefer?" the elderly gentleman asked. Looking at him for a brief moment, I answered "Point me towards the suits and you pick out two ties."

The elderly clerk motioned towards a rack of suits as he turned and walked away.

Knowing my jacket and pants sizes I picked out two dark blue suits. No sooner had I settled on the suits, than the clerk returned with two white shirts and two conservative ties.

"Sir, I estimated your shirt size 16 -16½ with 33-inch sleeve," replied the clerk. I smiled and said,

"Your estimation is spot on and the ties will do quite well."

As the clerk picked up the suits he asked "Are you Captain Allison Sir"?

"Yes, I am Byron Allison."

The clerk continued, "Senator Dial has made all the arrangements; will there be anything else?"

"No, that will be fine." I gathered up the parcels, and headed back to my room.

Chapter 14 - Funeral

We arrived at the McLelland estate at precisely six o'clock. We were met at the door by the butler. He greeted us both by name. He spoke with a shaky voice.

"Senator Dial, Mr. McLelland would like to see you in the study. He asked that I show you in as soon as you arrived. Captain Allison, Clay asked me to have you wait for him in the trophy room. If you'll go to your left through the sitting room and take the second door down the hallway."

"Thank you, James," I said. "How is Mrs. McLelland?"

"Not well sir," he said. "Not well at all."

He led Senator Dial away to the study and I headed towards the trophy room. I had been in the trophy room only once before and didn't really pay much attention. Looking around this time, I noticed that Clayton had a very large gun collection. Rifles, pistols, shotguns, all neatly displayed, some in glass-front cases and others in table-top glass cases. Moving from cabinet to cabinet I admired the guns. I walked over to the center of the room where a couple of glass cases sat atop a newly polished walnut table. The cases were unlocked and inside one was a matched pair of Ruger

GP 1000 .357 caliber Magnum Revolvers. Which was a fancy way of saying some big-ass handguns. The temptation was too great. I lifted the lid to the glass case and picked up one of the revolvers. I could tell it was loaded by the weight. I heard footsteps in the hall. I put the gun back and closed the case.

The door opened and Clay walked in. We both stood and stared at one another. After a moment I walked across the room and we embraced. Two warriors overwhelmed by our emotions and too proud to admit our pain. In that moment we formed a bond as close as two brothers.

That night and the next day had to be the worst twenty-four hours of my life. Mrs. McLelland looked like warmed-over death. She was never able to compose herself during the funeral and was constantly consumed by her tears. My heart went out to her. Clayton was almost in as bad a shape as his wife. No longer the towering rock of Gibraltar, instead he was a slump backed, beaten old man; his eyes were red and swollen from many tears and little sleep. Clay held up pretty well. It was plain to see it as a front.⁇ Someone had to stay strong during adverse times. As usual, Clay was the one.

Senator Dial and I were preparing to leave the cemetery when Clay walked over.

"Byron, can I talk to you?" he asked.

Dial took the cue and walked away.

"Byron, I found a letter in Tracy's room this morning," he was almost whispering. "It was addressed to me. Written the morning..." he hesitated, "written the morning she was killed. No, not killed," his voice rose, "not killed, *Murdered.*" Lowering his voice again, "She wrote it before leaving that morning.

92

Anyway, all she talked about in it was you. I don't know what happened between you two and," he put his hand up as if to stop me from saying anything, "I don't want to know, I don't care. But I wanted you to know that she loved you."

I looked at the ground. Then looked Clay in the eye. "I loved her too." I turned and headed toward Dial who was waiting in the parking lot.

"Byron, I have some business to attend to, Dial said on the way back to our hotel. "Do you think you'll be okay for a day or two? Don't worry about your room or anything of that sort. It'll continue to be paid for."

I think I can manage on my own for a couple of days," I said. "I have a few things I need to attend to."

"Good," said Dial. "Here are the keys to a rental car. You will find it in the parking deck of the hotel. The tag on the keys has its location." Senator Dial dropped me off at the hotel. I returned to my room, showered and went to bed.

The next morning, I went down to the hotel store and bought some toiletries, underwear, a couple pairs of slacks, a pair of jeans, two dark sweaters and a pair of lightweight gloves. After taking my new purchases to my room, I changed and headed to the parking deck to find the rental car. I drove back to the McLelland house to retrieve a few items I had left in my room and to talk with Clay. I pulled up in front of the house and exited the car. I didn't plan to be there very long. I left the car in the driveway and walked to the large front doors. Not wanting to bother anyone I didn't ring the doorbell, instead I opened the door and walked in. It seemed eerily quiet with none of the normal bustling around of the staff. I went straight to my room and found the small bag I had stored on the top shelf of the

93

closet. Leaving the bedroom, I quietly made my way to the Trophy room. After a few minutes alone, I left the room and headed to the kitchen to see if I could find anyone.

As I entered the dining room, I met James coming from the kitchen. As soon as he saw me, he straightened up sharply. James had been with the McLelland's, as their butler, for many years. It was obvious, from the look in his eyes, the loss of Tracy had affected the staff as well as the family. James spoke up.

"Captain Allison, sorry sir, I was just surprised to see you. Is there something we can get for you?"

"No thanks, James," I said. "I wanted to talk to Clay. Is he here?"

"No sir," replied James. "He left early this morning and said he would be gone perhaps a few days. Can I take a message?"

I thought it odd, Clay would leave for a few days at a time like this.

"No message, James," I said. "I will see him when he returns." Holding the small bag in one hand, I placed my other hand on James's shoulder.

Looking him straight in the eyes, I said "We all feel the loss." Turning, I walked back to the car

Chapter 15 - Shooting

Three days passed before I heard from the Senator again. I had almost decided that he had forgotten about me. It felt like the whole ordeal had been a dream. No, not a dream; a nightmare. In fact, if I wasn't holed up in a suite more lavish than I could ever afford and not having to pay the bill for, I would swear the whole thing was a dream. And at times I felt like they were going to barge in my room at any moment and accuse me of stealing the suite and throw me out on my ass. But that never happened.

The day that Dial came back to see me I had only been out of bed for about thirty minutes. Barely dry from my shower and wearing nothing but boxers and a t-shirt, I was startled by a banging on my door.

"Byron! Are you in there?" It was Dial. "Byron, open this door right now!"

I bolted for the door and flung it open. Dial stormed in the room, yelling about something I couldn't make any sense out of and waving a newspaper around.

"What the hell is wrong with you?" I yelled back. I shut the door before we could draw any more attention to ourselves.

"Byron," he said breathlessly, "I have tried to help you because I felt you were really a decent person. But there are some things I cannot condone!"

"Sir, I have no idea what you are talking about," I said.

"Two nights ago, were you in your room all night?"

"What are you trying to imply?" I realized that Dial was acting more out of fear than anger. He was more scared than upset.

He plopped the newspaper down on the table and pointed to the front page.

"There," he said. "Do you know anything about this?" he asked as he nearly collapsed in the chair.

I picked up the newspaper.

Indicted Man, Found Shot to Death

William Martin Crawford was found dead in his home yesterday morning. Details in the case are sketchy but investigators have ruled out burglary. Crime scene analysts put the time of death between ten and midnight on Monday. The fatal wound is consistent with a large caliber pistol. Crawford was under indictment for DUI and Vehicular Homicide in the death of Tracy McLelland, daughter of the wealthy, influential Clayton G. Mclelland Sr. Ms. Mclelland's brother, Clayton McLelland Jr. is being questioned and no charges have been filed, but officials are confident an arrest will be made soon.

I laid the paper back down on the table and sat in the chair across from Dial. I put my head in my hands.

"Byron," Dial was calm now. "You and Clay, one or both of you are involved in this. It has revenge written all over it. And I can have no part of this."

"What makes you think Clay or I were involved?" I said, "Is there anything connecting either of us?"

The Senator opened his mouth to respond, but the phone interrupted him.

I picked it up "Hello?" A voice I didn't recognize spoke.

"Could I speak to Captain Allison."

"Speaking," I said.

"Mr. Allison, this is Detective Anderson of the Vista View Police Department, I'm sorry to bother you during such trying times, but I am investigating the death of William Crawford and I would like to ask you a few questions."

"I have no objections to that, Detective," I said. "I was just leaving on my way to the McLelland's home. Should I come down to the station on my way or meet you somewhere?"

"Why don't I just meet you at the McLelland's home in an hour?" the detective said.

"I'll be there," I said and hung up the phone.

"Senator, if you could get me to the McLelland's house, I will leave you and get on with my life."

"I'll see that you get there." He said, "Meet me in the lobby in ten." He started to leave but stopped. "Once you get this matter cleared up, come back to Washington. We have some loose ends to tie up."

He left and I finished dressing, packed my bag and headed to the lobby. Senator Dial had a car waiting to take me to the McLelland house.

James met me at the McLelland's front door.

"Captain, Clay and the Detective are waiting for you in the trophy room."

"Thank you, James." I headed through the front room and down the hall. The trophy room door was open when I came to it.

"Come on in, Byron," Clay said. He was standing across the room at the window. The detective was sitting on the couch.

"This is Detective Anderson of our local police department."

Anderson stood and extended his hand. I shook it.

"Captain Byron Allison, pleasure to meet someone of your distinguished military honor," he said.

I didn't like him already.

"Well, I'll get right down to business," Andrews started. "Captain, have you ever been in this room before today?"

"On two occasions that I can recall," I said.

"Have you ever noticed the firearms in this room?"

"Yes, the gun collection is quite hard to miss," I said. I was starting to get irritated.

"Most specifically, have you noticed the collections of pistols?"

Now I was very irritated. "Again, they are quite hard to miss. Detective, if you are leading to something, I would appreciate it if you would come right out and say it."

"Oh, I wasn't leading to anything," he said. "I was just wondering if you had noticed that all the pistols were in matching pairs. Being a military man, I thought you might have noticed."

Damn, I thought. *I never noticed that they were all matched.* I knew I had seen the matched 357's but never noticed that every pistol was part of a pair. I casually walked over to the case where a few nights ago I had admired the two Ruger 357's. When I looked down in the case I almost choked. There lay a matched pair of Colt 45 automatics. No sign of the 357's. I glanced at Clay and he had a faint smile that was undetectable if you didn't know him. I looked back at the case.

"Alright, gentlemen," Anderson said. "Let's skip the bullshit. I've got a murdered stiff in the morgue and a boss that is eating my ass on this one. He's getting heat from upstairs and passing it down. Personally, I never liked this Crawford guy and his death is nothing to me.

But I have a job to do. Now I know everybody in this town and nobody has the skill to pull off a clean hit like this one.⯑ This was a professional hit. I've done a background check on both of you and either one of you could fit the profile.⯑ Right now, I cannot prove it one way or the other. But if I can pin it on one of you, your ass is mine. One of you will be hearing from me again. Soon I hope."⯑ He walked out.

I heard his footsteps all the way to the front door.⯑

I joined Clay at the window. We both gazed out over the back garden. He never asked me and I never asked him. And we both liked it that way.

Chapter 16 - MOH

I left the McLelland house and returned to the hotel. I needed to get to Washington D.C. There was the matter of my resignation from the Army and I needed to decide what I would do since the military was no longer an option. As I contemplated my next move, I realized, for all practical purposes, I was broke. As much as I hated asking for help, I called Senator Dial. After a couple of rings, Dial answered.

"Senator Dial, this is Byron Allison," I said.

"Byron, what can I do for you?" was Dial's reply.

"Senator, as much as I hate asking, I need some help returning to DC. I need to get the matter of my resignation and all the necessary paperwork completed." I continued, "Then I need to decide what I'm going to do with my life."

After a moment of silence, Dial replied "I've already left California, and back in DC, but I will contact Clayton and make arrangements for his plane to bring you to DC."

There was another uncomfortable moment of silence before Dial continued. "Once I talk to Clayton and all arrangements are made, someone will contact, you. Also, Byron, when you have formally been released from your military obligations, call me. I still would like to discuss your future with you."

Before I could say "thanks" the line when dead.

About 2 hours later, I received a phone call informing me that a car would be out front in 30 minutes to take me to the airport. I remember little of the flight to Washington D.C. I was exhausted and slept most of the way. The plane landed in DC several hours later. After landing the plane taxied to a small hangar where I departed. Once on the ground, I immediately saw an Army jeep with a rather sizable Staff Sergeant leaning against the hood. My first thought was he was there to arrest me. Realizing he didn't have a MP chevron on his sleeve, I headed his way.

Before I could say anything, the Sergeant spoke up. "Are you Captain Allison?"

I nodded and he continued. "I have orders to take you to the BOQ at Ft. Belvoir, Sir."

"Thank you, Sergeant" I said, as I pitched my bag into the back seat and settled in for the hour ride.

After arriving at the BOQ, I went in and registered. I learned a room had been reserved. The private behind the desk quickly shuffled my paperwork and handed me a key with directions to my room. As I entered the room, I was surprised to see my luggage laying on the bed. Someone was honest enough to get it delivered. I retrieved my uniform from the suitcase, hung it up, then undressed, showered and fell across the bed. The events of the last few days rolled through my head as I fell asleep.

The next few days were a blur. Getting out of the military was a more complicated process than getting in. The process included a de-briefing, spending several hours talking with a psychiatrist, a complete medical physical, a couple of hours in finance getting my back pay, a ton of paperwork and finally a session with a "Career Officer" discussing the many resources available in the effort to help adapting to civilian life. I was also informed I could remain at the BOQ for up to a week.

As I stepped out of the Career Officer's office I was approached by a courier. "Captain Allison," he said as he walked toward me.

Before he could continue, I corrected him.

"I'm now Mr. Allison."

"Sorry sir," he said as he smiled and handed me an envelope. "This is from Senator Dial's office, sir. I'm instructed to wait for a reply." I opened the envelope and read the content:

Captain Allison, your presence is requested at the Capitol Hill office of Senator Dial for a small reception in your Honor tonight at 7pm.

A car will pick you up at the BOQ at 6pm. You are also requested to wear your military uniform.

Unless otherwise notified, we look forward to seeing you.

Signed: ---- Senator Joseph Dial

I found it odd, Dial would request I wear my uniform knowing I was no longer in the military. I assured the courier I planned on attending. He thanked me before stating, "I will pass this information on to Senator Dial's office."

I stood motionless as the courier departed.

I arrived back at the BOQ with just enough time to shower, get my uniform in·order and be out front by the scheduled 6pm. As usual, a car and driver were waiting as I exited the building. We arrived at Senator Dial's office just a few minutes before 7pm. Since I didn't have a security badge to enter, the driver informed me, someone would be at the door to assist. I walked up the stairs as instructed. At the top of the steps, I was greeted by a well-dressed young lady. "Captain Allison, please follow me," she stated as she opened the large glass door.

Inside the glass doors were two security guards standing behind a large table. On the table, among several stacks of forms was a log in book.

One of the security guards asked to see my military ID card. Since I was no longer officially in the military, I no longer had the requested card! Before I could so state, the young lady chimed in. "Captain Allison is a personal guest of Senator Dial. "Log him in under my ID." She then turned and instructed me to sign the book. I complied. Again, she asked me to follow her.

She turned and headed down a large corridor leading to a bank of elevators. As we approached the elevators I spoke, "I don't believe we have been formally introduced." I smiled and continued, "You seem to know who I am, but I don't even know your name."

Before speaking she pressed a button on the panel. Turning she smiled and said, "My apologies, Captain.

My name is Malisa, I'm Senator Dial's Public Affairs Director."

Before I could reply, the elevator doors open. We entered with several others that had caught up with us. At the 7th floor, the doors opened and everyone, including myself exited.

I followed Malisa as we worked our way down a long corridor before stopping at a pair of large wooden doors. The plaque on the door read: Offices of Senator Joseph Dial. Before I could reach for the doors, Malisa opened one and motioned me in. I entered a large room bordered with chairs and a couple of small couches. The room was crowded with people I had never seen before. So much for a small reception, I thought. Malisa immediately started introducing me. At first, I tried to remember all the names being thrown at me. It was too many, too fast to succeed.

Amongst this crowd of humanity, I saw one face I recognized. Senator French of Alabama, he approached me with his hand extended. As we shook hands I started to apologize for the events of the past. He interrupted me.

"Captain Allison," he started. "I will be the first to admit, your actions of a few weeks ago pissed the hell out of me. However, after I was informed of the details leading up to your actions, I can say, I don't blame you and you have no cause to apologize. Now I can't say the same for the President," he laughed. "The President of the United States isn't accustomed to being stood up." French continued to chuckle. "Hell, he'll get over it in time. However, I wouldn't expect an invitation to the White House anytime soon, if I were you." With that, French gave out a loud chuckle. "At any rate," French went on, "I'm honored to be here tonight and speaking for the residents of the Great State of Alabama, we are all proud to welcome you home. I want you to know son," he continued, still holding my hand, "if you ever need anything, and I mean anything, all you need to do is contact my office. I stand behind you 100%." Before I could say thanks, he turned and was lost in the crowd.

Malisa appeared out of nowhere. She took my hand and whispered, "Come with me, Senator Dial would like to see you now."

Leading me across the room, she opened a door leading into a very ornate office. Standing at the window was Senator Dial and another man I didn't recognize. Malisa excused herself and exited the office. "Captain Allison," spoke Dial, as he approached me. Before he could continue, I interrupted.

"It's Byron Allison now, I'm no longer a Captain."

"Nonsense, Captain," Dial spoke up, "for the purpose of tonight, you are still a Captain in the United States Army." Before I could protest, Dial continued speaking. "At any rate, I have someone here I want you to meet." Turning, Dial motioned toward the man standing at the window.

"Captain Allison, I would like for you to meet Colonel JD Mathews."

"Captain Allison it's an honor and privilege to meet you." Mathews said as he shook my hand. "I've heard a lot about you and I'm quite impressed."

I thanked the Colonel as Dial instructed me to take a seat.

I took a seat along with Colonel Mathews. Dial looked at both of us before stating,

"Byron, Colonel Mathews would like to discuss a few matters with you before tonight's events. I'll give you guys a few minutes alone. Captain Allison, before I leave you alone with this old war dog," Dial and Mathews both laughed, as Dial went on, "don't make any type of decision before you and I talk. I have a proposal you might be interested in." Dial turned and walked out the door.

Colonel Mathews sat down.

"Byron, before I get started, I want you to know I'm familiar with the situation in California. I know Clayton and his family. Although I never met Tracy, I know she was a lovely young lady. I'm also aware of your relationship with her. I can only say I'm sorry for your and the McLelland family's loss. Not that it changes anything, but at least the bastard that caused this, got what he deserved." Reaching over and placing his hand on my shoulder, Mathews continued. "If I ever meet the person responsible for taking that son-of-a-bitch out, I would buy him the best bottle of cognac ever distilled." Smiling, Mathews looked me straight into the eyes before saying, "You do like cognac, do you not Captain?" Ignoring his question, I spoke.

"Colonel, you seem to know an awful lot about me."

Mathews chuckled before stating, "Byron, in my line of work, knowledge is more valuable than gold."

I asked, "And just what is your line of work?"

Mathews took a moment before speaking. "Captain, I'll skip the bullshit and get right to the point. I'm director of an organization that assists the Foreign Relations Department and the Department of Defense with facts finding and intel gathering. We can, at times, gather information in ways the military can't accomplish."

"In other words," I interjected, "You work for the CIA?"

Mathews hesitated a moment before continuing.

"I can't say who we actually report to, but suffice it to say, we have backing from the government."

I smiled for a second before adding, "I guess that answered my question."

"The point of me wanting to talk with you, Captain," Mathew went on to say, "we are always looking for people with your unique experience. You've proven yourself as a true leader. Someone that can be relied on to function with a clear head under extraordinary situations. I'm not asking you to make a decision tonight. I just wanted to let you know, we would be interested in meeting with you again sometime in the future, if you are so inclined. Plus, I know for a fact, Dial is going to offer you a position within his organization. A position, no doubt you are well suited for, but I'll let him go into that with you."

Just as I was about to ask more questions, the door opened and Senator Dial entered.

"I hate to interrupt," Dial chimed in, "but we have a lot of people starting to get antsy out here." Mathews stood, before saying "That's fine Senator, the Captain and I were just finishing up."

Turning to me, Mathew handed me a card, saying, "Captain, keep this card and call me anytime if ever you want to talk." Turning, Mathews exited the door.

"OK Captain," said Dial "If you will step out here, we will get the show on the road."

As I was about to exit the door, I started to ask Dial, *"what show!"* but I was interrupted by a loud applause from the room. Malisa appeared and directed me to a small open space in the otherwise crowded room. Senator French took a position on my left, Malisa on my right and Senator Dial standing off to my right a few feet away. Dial raised his hand and the room became quiet. Senator Dial began to speak.

"Captain Byron Allison, on behalf of a grateful nation and the President of the United States, you have been awarded the Congressional Medal of Honor for events that took place on or about January 30th 1968 in Cholon, Vietnam. The President of the United States regrets he wasn't available to present this medal personally. However, he has authorized me, Senator Joseph Dial, to present to you, Captain Byron Allison, our nation's highest military honor."

Stepping behind me, Dial reached around me, as he placed the blue, star covered ribbon supporting the Congressional Medal around my neck. Once around my neck, Dial then fastened the latch on the back. I understood now why I was requested to wear my uniform. However, I never expected this!

Before what was happening sank in, Dial stepped in front of me and said, "Captain Allison, as a past soldier, it is a great honor to be the first to salute you." As he raised his right hand into a very sharp military salute, I quickly returned his salute in as formal a salute as I could. Next thing I know, Malisa is reaching up to give me a kiss on the cheek. Before I could speak, people started filing in front of me with "Thank You" and "Congratulations." About all I could do was nod my head, smile and say Thank You in return. This went on far longer than I cared for, but I felt obligated. After all, these people did come out to see me receive this medal. Well, that and the free champagne.

When the final person stepped away, Malisa appeared again, and whispered, "Senator Dial would like to see you in his office, you can go right in."

Turning, I walked back to Dial's office and entered. Inside was Dial and a man I think I had met earlier tonight although I wasn't sure. "Byron," Dial quickly spoke up. "I would like you to meet Frank Givens. Frank is head of my personal security. My body guards so to speak." Frank stood and offered his hand. I shook it and we both sat down.

"Mr. Allison," Frank spoke up. "I've heard a lot about you and it's a pleasure to meet you. I've also read your dossier; quite impressive I might add."

I smiled before saying, "Seems a lot of people know a lot about me." He and Dial both laughed.

"Byron," Dial started, "Frank is getting ready to retire and we both think you might be the person to take his place."

Before Dial could continue, I spoke up. "Senator, I'm flattered and honored you think that way. But I don't know or have any experience in the field of personal security."

"Nonsense," it was Frank talking. "As a field officer in the Army, in every mission you completed, your primary objective was securing the safety of your men. This is no different. Granted, the landscape is different, but the objectives are the same. I will continue working in the background until you feel comfortable. Plus, there's a training course we will send you through. The course is "Practices, Protocol and Policies" for personal security personnel. Along with that is a course in firearm safety and procedure. The same courses all Secret Service personnel attend. With your experience, you'll not have a problem with any of the training. Again, I will be around to guide you."

This time it was Dial speaking up. "Byron, I'm a pretty good judge of people. I truly believe you are the man for this task." He smiled before continuing. "You might even say, I'm willing to bet my life on it."

I gave that statement a moment of thought before speaking. "Senator, it's not like I have a lot of options on the table. I've just been released from the Army with no plans for the future. I would need some time to find a place to live, most of my clothes are military and I don't own a vehicle."

Before I could continue, Dial spoke, "Let me take care of that."

The expression on my face must have expressed my doubt. Continuing, Dial explained. "We maintain an apartment here in DC. A government issued car is part of the position. As far as the clothing, I can send you to a men's shop and they will handle that. We can discuss payment after your salary gets started. See Byron, we have eliminated all your excuses." He and Frank both laughed. We all sat in silence for what felt like a long period.

Finally, I stood and extended my hand to Dial before saying, "You are right Senator, you are betting your life on me. I will do all within my power to see you don't lose that bet."

Chapter 17 - New Career

The next 4 weeks were hectic to say the least. My apartment was a nice, if not small, one bedroom flat on a side street in an upper scale neighborhood. I spent the first day getting situated in my new living quarters. A quick trip to a grocery store and I had the basics of nutrients. I was either attending different training courses or I was working with Frank. The training courses were fairly straightforward firearms training and safety was basic military. I breezed through the course and qualified top of the class. The course title "Policy, Procedures and Protocol" was a little different. I managed to qualify in the upper half. This course covered the policies governing a government bodyguard: when to draw your weapon, how to handle confrontations, and how to stay behind the scenes while remaining in the forefront. In other words, how to be invisible and still scan any crowds or groups for potential problems. The number one objective of a government body guard is to protect the client at all costs. The instructors stressed continuously; a body guard must do whatever necessary to ensure no harm is bestowed upon the client.

Being a bodyguard and worse, being in charge of five other bodyguards is not an easy task. However, the staff were very well trained and disciplined. They knew their job and performed it with great precision. Any time Senator Dial was scheduled to be out in public, at least four of us were with him. I learned from Frank, in addition to making sure we were properly staffed, my primary function placed me the closest to Dial. In case of any type disturbance, it was the staff's function to deal with incidents. My role was to ensure the safety of Senator Dial.

This being an election year, Dial's schedule was hectic. During the first months, he made one or two public appearances a week. Each engagement went off without a hitch. I realized quickly how easy it would be to become complacent. That was a point Frank and the course instructors elaborated on. Never assume anything. All it takes is one disgruntled person to turn a friendly crowd into a disaster.

On this particular day we had flown to a small town in southern California, just outside San Diego. Senator Dial was part of a small group of California politicians addressing a gathering of supporters. Being the state's senator, Dial was the keynote speaker and scheduled to take the podium last. This was my first outing without Frank present. As Senator Dial was being introduced, I made a radio check to the other bodyguards. A quick reply from each assured me all was normal. I moved a little closer to the podium as Dial stood from his chair. Just as Senator Dial started walking across the stage my radio roared alive with the words:

"Gun, Gun, Gun!"

Without hesitation or giving the situation any thought, I bolted toward Dial. I distinctly remember hearing the first shot just as I slammed into Senator Dial like an offensive lineman would hit a quarterback. Three or four other shots rang out in what sounded like one big bang. Somewhere between lunging toward the Senator, knocking him to the stage floor and covering his prostrate body with mine, I felt a sharp, hot pain in my left thigh. Dial was trying to speak but I couldn't make out his words due to the radio traffic I was receiving in my ear piece.

"Perpetrator down, perpetrator down, perpetrator shot and down" were the first words to be broadcasted through my headset. Then I heard, "Threat eliminated; area secure."

It was at that moment I realized I was trying to lift my left arm to reply. As hard as I tried, my arm wouldn't move.

By now the stage was crawling with security personnel. I rolled to my right off of Senator Dial and attempted to get to my feet just as the other guards arrived. Dial, seemingly undeterred by the whole situation, kneeled at my side.

"Byron", Dial was saying, "Stay down, you are shot."

"Are you OK," I replied, still trying to get my feet under me.

"I'm fine, son," Dial continued "Medical personnel are on the way."

Suddenly I felt very tired.

I vaguely became aware of one of the EMTs asking where I was shot. Before I could reply, I felt another medical member cutting the leg of my pants. The last thought I had before I passed out, *"Damn, that's my new suit."*

I don't remember anything after that. I became vaguely aware of my surroundings in a hospital room. I noticed my left leg was slightly elevated and my left arm was in a sling. As I was looking around a nurse entered the room.

"Mr. Allison!" she exclaimed. "You are awake!"

I was aware I was in pain. In my mind, I didn't really care. I was trying to muster the energy to speak as the nurse inserted a needle into my IV. As she did, she smiled and said, "This will make you feel better."

My mind went blank!

I later learned, for the next four days they kept me sedated not wanting me to move my shoulder and arm. The gun shot in my leg, although serious, wasn't as concerning as the one in my shoulder. The first bullet penetrated the back of my thigh without hitting bone or an artery. It appeared the second bullet hit some part of the podium slowing it down. However, upon impact with the soft wood of the podium, the projectile mushroomed somewhat and was embedded with wood fibers. These tiny particles of contamination were the real issue. As serious as the wound was, the doctors were more concerned about the possibility of infection. They were fearful that any movement of the arm could cause these minuscule fragments of wood to reach deeper into the muscle.

On the fourth day I started becoming more aware of my situation. I opened my eyes as a nurse was removing the bandage from my shoulder.

"Mr. Allison," the nurse said, smiling. "The doctor will be here in a few minutes to examine your wounds. I suspect he will want to talk to you as well."

Before I could reply, the door opened and the doctor along with another nurse entered.

"Well, good morning, how's our hero today?" the doctor said with a chuckle.

"I'm doing great," I said, trying to muster some enthusiasm and failing. "When can I leave?"

Examining my shoulder, the doctor continued. "We plan to keep you here a few more days, possibly a week or so. Then you will need some extensive physical therapy."

"Doc, I really need to get out of here," I said with a bit more enthusiasm. "I have things I need to be doing."

I'm not sure what it was I needed to be doing, but in my mind, I felt there was something.

Looking up from the shoulder, and with a sterner voice the doctor replied, "Mr. Allison, it will take a while before you will be able to walk unassisted. Also, at this point you have little or no use of your arm. Hell man," he went on without taking a breath, "I doubt you could even wipe your own ass at this stage."

The two nurses giggled as the thought of what he was saying sent chills down my back.

"Tomorrow," the doctor kept talking, "we will get you up and let you take a few steps. This is going to be a slow process. You have two serious wounds. I expect a full recovery if you follow the proper instructions."

The second nurse started re-bandaging my shoulder as the other nurse pulled the sheet down. After removing my bandage, and examining the leg the doctor turned back to me.

"Mr. Allison, you are a very lucky man, if you can call being shot, lucky. As serious as the wounds are, the bullets didn't strike anything vital. A week or so here, a month of physical therapy and you will be at 75% to 80% recovered. The remainder will come over time. A year from now, you won't even know you were shot. The wounds seem to be stable and again, I anticipate a full recovery. We will be cutting back on your pain medications. If the pain gets too bad, let someone know and we will re-examine the level of the meds. I don't want you getting dependent on any drugs."

With that, all three left the room.

That evening, Senator Dial and Frank came by. With the reduced level of drugs being administered, my mind was a lot clearer.

"Byron, I can't thank you enough for your actions," were the first words from Senator Dial. "I would not be here today except for your fast thinking."

"I was doing what was expected of me," I stated. "Did anyone else get injured?"

"No one with the exception of the perpetrator," Frank spoke up. "He was eliminated quickly. We are still investigating his motive," Frank continued. "It appears he was acting alone."

Senator Dial spoke up. "Byron, there are no words that can express my true gratitude. However, what I can do is to make sure you receive the best medical care this country has to offer. I've already filed the necessary paperwork to ensure you are taken care of financially. You will continue to draw your full salary for the next 12 months. At which time and assuming you are fully recovered, you will have a choice. You can return working for the government in some very similar capacity or you can elect to retire. Should you choose retirement, you will receive 70% of your present salary with full medical benefits."

Dial stopped and took a deep breath before continuing. "If you ever, and I mean ever, need anything, all you have to do is contact me or anyone on my staff."

Dial reached into his pocket and removed a card with two phone numbers written on it.

"Byron, I'm going to lay this card here," Dial said, indicating a place on the table. "The first number is for a car service. I've spoken with them and they know the situation. If and when you need transportation, just give them a call. They are available 24/7 and as often as you need. The second number is for the Hyatt downtown. It was decided, when you leave the hospital, you would be better served in a hotel than your apartment. The doctors have explained to us, your mobility will be limited. Especially using your injured arm. Again, they have been made aware of the situation."

It was Frank's turn to speak. "Byron, we don't want you to get the feeling you are alone. Myself, Senator Dial and our staff will be checking on you. We understand you have no immediate family. Half of the United States Senate has become your family."

"What's most important," Senator Dial interjected, "is your health, well-being and a speedy recovery."

Both men turned and headed to the door. Senator Dial stopped and turned before saying.

"Byron, I owe you my life. I will be keeping tabs on you to make sure all is well." He smiled and walked out.

Chapter 18 - Hospital Visits

The next day after Dial's visit, I was transferred to another floor of the hospital. I was placed in a private room on the Physical Therapy ward. The following weeks proved to be very tiring. Physical therapy twice a day. One session for my leg and the other for my shoulder/arm. Plus, this facility didn't take the weekends off. Seven days a week they had me up and walking. At first it was very demanding. The pain wasn't as much an issue as the isolation I felt. For the first time in my life, I felt alone. As much as I hated to admit it, my situation was having an effect on my mental attitude. With the exception of my two therapy sessions a day, I did nothing but lay in my room.

One morning about three weeks into my daily workouts, I heard a commotion in the hall outside my room. I heard a voice I recognized, telling someone: "I told you I am immediate family, Byron is my brother."

Then the nurse spoke up saying: "We are told Mr. Allison has no immediate family and you can't be allowed in his room."

The door to my room opened as Clay, walking backwards with the nurse right in his face, interrupted the nurse mid-sentence. "Byron tells people he doesn't have a brother."

Before the now frustrated nurse could respond, Clay turned facing me and said "Byron, tell this pretty nurse the truth, tell her I'm your brother."

Laughing, I looked at the nurse and said, "It's ok, no doubt, he's my brother."

Before turning and storming out of the room, the nurse angrily said, "This is bullshit, I'm reporting both of you."

Clay grabbed a chair and slid it up closer to the bed. "Well, brother, other than being surrounded by pretty nurses, how are things?"

Before I could reply Clay continued, "Senator Dial was at the house a few days ago and explained what happened. In his eyes you are a hero. Of course, we already knew that. Mom and Dad send their best. Dad said, if you need anything just let him know. He also wanted me to tell you, if you would like to come to the house while you are recovering, he will send the plane for you."

Finally getting a word in, I smiled and said, "Tell your mom and dad I appreciate the offer. Once I'm released and can get around, I plan to head back to Alabama and get my life sorted out. I'm not sure how long it will take to get back to full recovery. The doctors assure me it will happen. By the way, how's your mom? I've been thinking about her and the overall situation."

Clay sat motionless for a moment before replying. "She's having a hard time. The doctor kept her sedated for over a week, but it was decided any longer could present problems of its own. She rarely goes outside the house. The doctor assures us she will be ok in the long run and has to deal with this in her own way. Dad has arranged for a psychologist to start working with her. Hopefully we will start seeing an improvement."

It was my turn to reflect before asking, "You heard anything from that detective? I can't remember his name."

"Detective Anderson." Clay replied before continuing. "I understand he's been asking around interviewing everyone he might think has any knowledge of the dead guy." Clay smiled before continuing, "I can't remember his name."

"William Crawford," I said.

"Right, William Crawford." Clay more spit out the name than spoke it. "Dad had an attorney look into the investigation. According to this attorney, Anderson has hit a dead end. However, Anderson is quoted as saying he knows who whacked the dude, but he can't prove it – yet."

We sat in silence a few minutes before Clay stood and with a serious look on his face started whispering. "Byron, I'm not cut out for the corporate world. Dad has tried to ease me into the family business. He and I both know it's not working out. Senator Dial has offered me a position on his security staff. Not as your replacement, but just part of the staff. Dial has also offered to introduce me to a fellow named Mathews. I believe he said Mathews was a retired Army Colonel.

Dial mentioned you have met this Colonel. I've got a grasp on what Colonel does, but what is your opinion?"

"Colonel Mathews," I began, "runs some type of Black Ops operation. Since he's affiliated with Dial, I can only assume he is connected in some manner with the CIA. However, that is speculation on my part. According to the meeting I had, Mathews contended his operation is purely recon. He did indicate the reconnaissance carries a certain level of combat risk. During this same meeting, Mathews gave me his card and said if I was ever interested in talking further to give him a call."

Clay seemed to be in deep thought before asking, "Have you considered giving him a call?"

"I toyed with the idea," I continued, "before accepting Senator Dial's offer to head up his security staff and look what that got me. Are you thinking about contacting him?"

Clay hesitated before answering. "I have given it some thought. I tried to question Dial about Mathews but all he said was, give Matthew a call and let him answer your questions. I have some loose ends to tie up with the business and with dad before I can do anything. I just wanted your advice and opinion before making any decision."

"Changing the subject," I said, "what about your political aspirations? Your dad practically had you running for President."

We both laughed before Clay replied. "Dad and I had a long conversation over his plans for me. We both agreed I should follow whatever course I choose. Dad understands, he can't make life choices for me. No doubt he will support any decision I make. Dad and

Senator Dial have been close friends for many years. Their friendship goes back to when Dial was an unheard-of candidate running for County Commissioner. I'm fairly confident that any conversation I have with Senator Dial, Dad's aware of."

Clay looked at his watch before continuing. "Byron, I need to leave. The jet is scheduled to depart in an hour. Let me know when you get back home."

Clay extended his hand and I took it. "Take care my friend," I said, as Clay nodded. Releasing my hand from his tight grip, he turned and left the room.

I laid in bed trying to decide what I needed to do. I wasn't sure, but I knew whatever it was, it didn't include staying here in the hospital. By now I could walk with a limp and as limited as it was, I could use my left arm. Turning slightly to my right I reached over and retrieved the card Senator Dial left on the bed stand. Picking up the phone, I dialed the number for the car service. It rang twice before someone answered.

"Patriot Car Service," came the voice of a young lady.

"My name is Byron Allison," I spoke into the phone. "Senator Joseph Dial instructed me to call your service if I needed a car and driver." I had learned really fast, dropping Senator Dial's name is a quick way to get things done.

"Yes Mr. Allison," the young lady responded. "We have you listed in the database. What can we do for you today?"

"I need a car and driver sent to," I hesitated trying to remember the hospital name, "a car and driver sent to the St. Vincent hospital." Finally remembering the name. "I will also need the driver for several hours. Please ask the driver to come to room 614. I may need a little assistance."

"Certainly Mr. Allison, we can have a car there in an hour, if that's acceptable," the young lady answered.

"An hour will be fine, thank you," I said.

I laid the phone back on its cradle and started getting out of bed. It was at that moment I panicked. I realized I didn't have any clothes. There I stood in my hospital gown, my bare ass showing in the back. I slid the drawer open on the bedside table and was relieved to see my billfold. Satisfied my credit cards were intact, I counted my cash. Two hundred odd dollars. OK, that issue is resolved, now how to get pants, shirt and shoes.

About 40 minutes later, I heard a knock on the door.

"Come in," I said.

In walked a familiar looking individual. It took me a moment to put his face to a name. Before I could say anything, he extended his hand and said,

"Captain Allison, it's good to meet you again. I'm Anthony Danley, formally Master Sergeant Danley. We met some time back in Washington, DC."

Shaking his hand, I smiled and said, "Master Sergeant Danley, you are an answer to a prayer. You have a way of being at the right place at the right time, for saving my ass."

Danley laughed and said, "I happened to be in the office when you called. As soon as I heard your name, I told the dispatcher I wanted this assignment. What adventure are we about to get into?"

"First, I stated, I'm no longer a Captain. My name is Byron. Second, I want to leave the hospital and I have no clothes. I need you to go get me a pair of pants, a shirt and some form of shoes."

Before I could continue, Danley spoke up. "Sir, oh, I mean Byron, we always carry an extra change of clothes. I have a small suitcase in the car and I believe we are close enough in size, the clothes should fit well enough to get you out of here. Also, like you, I'm no longer military. Call me Anthony."

I looked at the clock on the wall. "OK, Anthony," I said, "we have less than an hour before someone comes to take me to physical therapy. If we are going to make it out of here it needs to be done quickly."

Without saying a word, Anthony turned and exited the room.

Picking up the phone, I fished a phone number out of my billfold. I dialed the number quickly and heard "Hello." Taking a deep breath, I spoke.

"Clay, this is Byron."

"Hey buddy," came the reply, "is everything OK? What can I do for you?"

"Clay," I started, "I need to get out of California and back to Alabama. Any chance your plane is headed back east in the near future?"

"They are releasing you from the hospital?" Clay asked.

"Well," I replied, "Let's just say I'm releasing myself."

"I understand," Clay said as he laughed. "Byron, the plane won't be available until about mid-day tomorrow. I can have it fueled and ready by about 1PM. Will that work?"

"That will work fine," I said with a sigh of relief.

"You need anything else?" Clay added.

"Clay", I continued, "I can't thank you and your family enough."

A chuckle came over the phone before Clay spoke. "Don't worry about it. I have your back just like you have mine." The line went dead, just as Anthony entered the room carrying a small black overnight bag.

"OK Byron," Anthony said as he unzipped the bag. "These clothes may not fit you like a glove. But they will cover your bare ass and get you out of here."

I took the pair of dark pants he handed me and put them on. At this point I wasn't concerned with underwear. He was right about the size. They were loose and baggy. I tighten the belt as far as possible. The shirt was the same. At least one size too large. I struggled to button up the light blue shirt. Anthony set a pair of black loafers on the floor. Sliding a foot into the first shoe I realize they too were a size too large.

I stood for a moment before speaking. "I sure hope we don't have to run."

Anthony laughed. "Hopefully that won't be necessary." He asked, "Where are we headed?"

"We are going to the Hyatt," I answered. "However, we need to find a place where I can get some clothes that fit. Nothing fancy, just a pair or two of jeans and a couple of T-shirts."

"And shoes," Anthony said with a chuckle.

I nodded my head in agreement.

I instructed Anthony to look out the door and see if the hall was clear. Picking up the bag, he peered out the door. Not saying a word, Anthony raised his thumb.

"Go to the elevator and get the door open and I will follow," I said.

I waited a couple of seconds before walking out into the hall. With a quick glance around, I made my way to the elevators, trying my best not to limp. Anthony was holding the elevator door open as I approached. Once in the elevator, Anthony released the door and pressed the button for the ground floor.

The lobby of the hospital was crowded with people coming and going. As we exited, Anthony picked up a newspaper lying on an end table.

Handing it to me, he said "Take this paper, have a seat and cover your face. I will get the car and drive it around to the door."

Taking the paper, I sat down near the door and raised the paper as though I was reading it. I sat staring at the paper until I saw Anthony drive up to the front door. Looking around quickly, I rose and headed out the door. Just as I was exiting the second of the two double doors leading outside, I met the afternoon physical therapist coming in.

"Mr. Allison!" she exclaimed. What are you doing down here?" She looked around before continuing, "and alone too! You aren't supposed to leave the floor and certainly not without assistance."

I saw Anthony open the passenger door, as the therapist continued.

"Mr. Allison, have you considered what would happen if you fell?" I looked at the therapist as I spied Anthony.

"Ma'am, you are absolutely correct," I stated. "In fact, I'm feeling a bit queasy, perhaps I need a wheelchair."

With a look of horror, the therapist said. "You stay right here, don't you move! I will run inside and get a wheelchair and get you back to the floor."

The nurse launched forward as I moved to the car as fast as my bad leg would allow. Anthony helped me in and quickly closed the door. Sprinting around the hood of the car, Anthony jumped in and put the automobile in drive all in one motion. As we pulled away from the door, I saw the therapist emerge pushing a wheelchair. Through the side mirror I could see her looking frantically for me.

"OK Byron," Anthony spoke with a chuckle, "where to now?"

"First things first," I said. "Find a clothing store. Nothing fancy, just some jeans and a couple of T-shirts."

A quick stop at a Sears and Roebuck and my wardrobe was intact. Once back in the car, I asked Anthony to drive to the Hyatt. We rode in silence for a while before I spoke.

"Anthony, if I remember correctly, you have a son in the Army, infantry, I believe."

"Yes," Anthony quickly spoke. "He's scheduled to be discharged next month. After his second tour in Nam, I thought he might stay in."

"Decided not to make a career like his old man?" I asked.

"Yeah, and I can't fault him," Anthony answered. "The military has changed so much since my early days. I was part of the first advisory team Kennedy sent to Vietnam. Back then the military was run by the military. Nowadays, it's run by a bunch of suit and tie politicians." He hesitated before continuing. "Sorry sir, didn't mean to start carrying on."

"No problem," I chimed in, "I totally agree with you. You said your son's name is Tony?"

"Yes sir, Tony. His mother wanted to name him Anthony, like his dad. I didn't want a *junior* so we compromised with Tony."

"What's Tony going to do once he's discharged?" I asked.

"He's not 100% sure," Anthony said. "I suggested he look into the GI Bill pertaining to furthering his education. He and I were talking the other night and he mentioned he was contacted about doing some contract work. He was vague on the details. It seems there's some outfit recruiting prior military personnel. Doing what, he wasn't sure."

I immediately thought about Colonel Mathews, but chose to keep it to myself.

"Anthony," I said as we arrived at the hotel. "Would you care to hang around for dinner? I understand you have family and if you need to get home, just say so." Before I could finish, Anthony spoke up with a laugh.

"You know Byron, this is just like the military. Here's an old sergeant making sure an officer doesn't get into trouble. You seem to have a knack for getting your ass in a sling. I want to hang around and see what happens next."

I laughed this time as I slowly exited the car.. Anthony pitched the keys to the valet. We waited for the receipt and then entered the hotel lobby.

A pretty young lady quickly greeted us at the desk.

"Good evening gentlemen, what can I do for you tonight."

I smiled. "My name is Byron Allison," I started. "I was informed by Senator Joseph Dial that you had a room waiting for me."

The young lady started typing on the computer. After a moment she looked up and still smiling, said, "Ye,s Mr. Allison, we have been expecting you. We have a suite on the 6th floor if that is acceptable."

I glanced over to Anthony before replying.

"The 6th floor is fine. We will be requiring room service. Can I place an order with you?"

The clerk reached under the counter and retrieved a form. "Yes sir," she said. "What can we prepare for you gentlemen?"

"We will have two of your best porterhouse steak,s" I said. Looking back at Anthony, I continued, "medium rare, baked potatoes and a garden salad, ranch dressing." Anthony nodded with approval.

"Will there be anything else?" the clerk asked.

"Yes," I said. "I would like a bottle of Crown Royal, Black."

"Sir," the clerk spoke up. "I'm not sure we have Crown Royal, Black."

I turned facing the clerk, propped my arms on the counter before replying. "Perhaps the concierge can locate one." The clerk, never once losing her smile, said, "I'm sure he can. Will you need any mixers, water or ice?"

"Heaven forbid," I said. "And ruin a good Canadian Blended Whiskey?"

The clerk's face turned a slight reddish glow.

"I'm sorry sir, she almost whispered. "I'm not much of a whiskey drinker." I smiled before saying, "OK, we'll forgive you this time."

I heard Anthony chuckle behind me.

After signing the required form, the clerk handed me a key card.

Anthony and I walked to the elevator. Once the door opened and we entered, Anthony jokingly said, "Saving the big man's life sure seems to have its privileges."

"Trust me," I replied. "I could do without the so-called privileges. All I want is to get out of this town and back to Alabama."

"And what are you going to do once you get back home?" asked Anthony.

"To be honest," I replied, "I haven't the faintest idea, but I will take my slow and easy time figuring it out."

Before I could say anything else, the doors opened. Anthony and I walked to the room.

It wasn't long after we entered the room that I heard a knock on the door. Before I could get out of the chair, Anthony jumped up. Standing just outside the door was a young man holding a large bottle of Crown Royal, Black. Anthony tipped the fellow and closed the door.

Looking at me, he said, "I don't know about you, but I sure could use a drink right now." I nodded and Anthony poured us a drink.

Just as we settled in our chairs, came another knock on the door. I motioned to Anthony to remain seated. This time I opened·the door. "Room service," said the attendant pushing in a cart.

"Just leave the cart over by the table," I instructed. "We can handle it from there."

I handed the attendant a twenty-dollar bill. He thanked me and left.

The dinner was every bit as good as I had hoped. I realized I hadn't eaten all day. Anthony made short work of his meal as well.

Once finished and refilling our drink glasses, Anthony and I moved back to the more comfortable arm chairs.

"Anthony," I said, "earlier you asked me what I was going to do once I arrived home. The first thing is to get myself back into shape. I'm still several months away from being able to do anything strenuous. But with some hard physical training, I know I can do it. Hell, I've done it before. Once that's out of the way, as I see it, I have a couple of options. Like your son, I too have been contacted by an organization about doing some contract work. Again, like Tony was telling you, the details are sketchy. I might choose to research this operation a bit farther."

We sat in silence a few moments before Anthony spoke. "Damn, Byron, if you pursue the contract work and Tony follows suit, it's conceivable the two of you could cross paths."

"It's certainly possible," I agreed.

"It's really not likely," Anthony added. "But if it was to happen, do me a favor and keep an eye on him. Don't get me wrong, I'm not asking for any special treatment, just to keep an eye on him." Anthony paused and cleared his throat before continuing. "He's my only son if you know what I mean."

Anthony and I spent the best part of the night drinking whiskey and telling war stories. Around 2am I told Anthony I had to lay down. Even with the alcohol consumption, my shoulder and leg were hurting. I explained I would need a ride to the airport tomorrow as well. I suggested he take the extra bedroom. He didn't hesitate to accept my offer.

Chapter 19 - Leaving Town

I was up just after sunrise for no other reason than my leg and shoulder was still hurting. I realized, while in the hospital, they were still giving me something for pain. I knew this was something I was going to have to deal with.

I showered, dressed and made a pot of coffee. I was on the phone ordering Anthony and me breakfast when I heard the shower in the other room. I knew Anthony was up. Not long after, he came out of the bedroom drying his hair.

"There's coffee," I said as Anthony walked to the counter. "Thanks," he replied. "I need a strong cup." After pouring himself a cup, Anthony took a sip and pulled up a stool before continuing.

"What's on the agenda for today? You mentioned, last night, you needed a ride to the airport. I assume you are leaving California; will you be returning?"

"Not for a while, if ever," I said. "I need to get in some decent physical shape and I figure I can do that best back home. What comes next will be decided at a later date."

Before Anthony could reply, there was a knock on the door. Anthony rose and opened the door. An attendant rolled a cart in with our breakfast. I signed the tab as Anthony started uncovering the food. We ate in silence, each consumed in our own thoughts. Once we had our fill of eggs benedict, sausage, fresh fruit and toast, I broke the quietness.

"I don't need to be at the airport for a couple of hours. However, I want to disappear. You and I are the only two that know where I'm headed. Once I get to the airport, I can relax in the lounge. Did I mention, we aren't going to the main concourse? We will be going to a private hanger."

Anthony stood and took the last sip of coffee from his cup.

"I'll get the car brought around and meet you downstairs." At that, he left. I gathered my meager wardrobe of recent Sears and Roebuck purchases and headed downstairs.

Anthony was waiting with the car when I walked out of the Hyatt. I got into the passenger side as he put the car in gear. The ride to the airport took about 45 minutes. Lucky for me, Anthony knew how to get to the private hangars. As we approached the gate entrance, Anthony slowed. I realized neither of us had spoken a word the whole trip.

"Hangar 426," I said, as we passed through the gate. Anthony pulled the car up to a side door with a large 426 on the hangar. Before opening the door, I uncomfortably turned slightly and extended my right hand.

"Anthony," I sighed, "I can never thank you enough. If you ever need anything, or need any help, I'm a phone call away." With that I shook his hand and handed him my phone number.

Anthony chuckled before replying. "I may look you up someday. You be safe Captain, and watch your six."

Picking up my Sears and Roebuck bag, I exited the car.

As Anthony pulled away, I entered the hangar. I didn't realize how large this structure was. I saw four small to midsize jets with two more sitting just outside the double sliding doors. I made my way across the building to a door marked, *Office*. Entering the office, I was greeted by a man sitting at a desk. He looked up and spoke.

"Good morning, can I help you?"

"Yes," I replied, "my name is Byron Allison. I'm supposed to be boarding a plane owned by Clay McLelland."

The man at the desk retrieved a clipboard and shuffled a few pages before replying. "Yes, Mr. Allison, I have you on the list. The plane hasn't arrived, but is due in an hour or less. According to the manifest, it is scheduled to be fueled before departing."

I felt relieved.

"I realize I'm early," I said. "Is there a place I can wait?"

"Yes sir," the man said, hanging the clipboard back on the wall before continuing. "Through that door," indicating a door behind him, "there's fresh coffee and a place to relax. Someone will notify you when it's time to board."

I thanked him and headed to the other door. I entered a nicely decorated lounge with several chairs, a small bed and a recliner. Getting a cup of coffee, I sat down.

Sipping on the coffee, I started thinking about this past several months. Then mentally I started analyzing my life.

Being a young boy in the backwoods of Alabama was a great way to grow up. We lived less than a half mile from my grandparents. My grandmother was the typical southern grandmother. It didn't matter what time of the day or night, when you walked into her kitchen, there was a plate of biscuits sitting on the counter. They might be hot or left over, but they were always a great snack for a growing boy. She passed away when I was 9 years old. To this day I still miss her biscuits and gravy. My grandfather was just as typical of a grandfather as of the times. Hard working, family oriented, patriarch. He had perhaps a 6th grade education, but was one of the smartest men I've ever known.

My dad worked at a local machine shop and to my knowledge never missed a day's work. Dad served in the Army during WWII. He was part of the invasion force at Normandy on D-Day. He never spoke about this time in his life. Truth be known, it was what he never said that influenced me and made me want to join the Army. Mother was a stay-at-home mom as were most moms of the day.

When I was 13 years old, my parents were returning home from visiting my dad's brother. An approaching car crossed the centerline and hit them head on. Both of my parents and the other driver were killed. It was rumored the other driver was drinking. My life changed drastically. I lived with my grandfather for the next few years. I was offered a football scholarship from a local college. Not only did I play football, but I managed to excel in ROTC. Upon my graduation, I joined the Army.

I was thinking of the fun my grandfather and I used to have hunting and fishing in the backwoods, when suddenly I became aware of a voice.

"Mr. Allison, Mr. Allison, sorry to disturb your sleep, but your flight is ready to depart." I looked around to realize a gentleman was standing beside the recliner still talking. "Sir, they've just finished fueling and will be ready to leave in a few minutes."

Almost jumping to my feet, I thanked the man and headed out the door. Just outside I was greeted by one of the pilots.

"Mr. Allison, glad to have you joining us today. Mr. McLelland has briefed us on your trip." Reaching for my Sears and Roebuck bag, he continued, "Go ahead and board. Take a seat and as quickly as we get airborne, I can give you an ETA."

Handing him my bag, I ascended the couple of steps into the jet and took a seat. A few moments later, the pilot boarded, closed the door and stepped into the cockpit. I felt the plane start to move as we taxied away from the hangar. Just as the plane turned onto the runway, I heard the engines rev up as the thrust pushed us forward. In just a matter of seconds, we were off the ground and headed into the clouds. Once we leveled out, the pilot came from the cockpit into the seating area.

"Mr. Allison," he said. "Again, welcome aboard." Before I could comment he continued. "We will be cruising at 28,000 ft. Weather is expected to be mild and clear. Our flight time to Birmingham, Alabama is expected to be just over 4 hours. We are expecting a tail wind so we could be there in a little less time. If you care for anything, we have snacks and drinks in the galley," indicating with his right hand. "The bathroom is located in the rear of the plane." This time indicating with his left hand. "Sit back, relax and enjoy the flight." With that, the pilot smiled and returned to the cockpit.

I remember very little of the flight. I dozed off and the next thing I remember was the pilot touching my arm saying, "Mr. Allison, we will be touching down in approximately 10 minutes. Weather is clear and the temperature is around 85F."

"Thank you," I said.

As the pilot returned to the cockpit, the plane landed right on time. It was a short taxi to the hangar. Once the plane stopped and the door opened, I exited. Standing outside was a man holding my Sears and Roebuck bag. Looking at me with a sideways smile, he said:

"Mr. Allison, I presume."

"Yes, I'm Byron Allison," I said as I reached for my Sears and Roebuck bag.

"My name is Tom. I was told you might need a car and driver. I have a car waiting to take you home, or wherever you need to go."

It was at that very moment I realized what a great friend Clay was. In my haste to get home, I had never considered what I was going to do once I reached the airport. I'd made no arrangements. Here I am, standing on the tarmac of a private hangar, 30 miles from my house, a limited amount of cash in my pocket, and my belongings in a Sears and Roebuck bag...which Tom has yet to give me.

"Tom," I said. "A ride to my house would be greatly appreciated."

Still holding my Sears and Roebuck bag, Tom gestured to a dark sedan and said, "This way Mr. Allison, once we get outside the gate you can give me directions."

I followed Tom to his car. Quickly we were out the gate and headed to my house. The drive to the house took about 40 minutes. Traffic was light and it was just starting to get dark when we arrived. I exited the car and thanked Tom. He smiled and handed me my Sears and Roebuck bag.

"Traveling kind of light, aren't you Mr. Allison?" Tom said with a laugh.

Taking my bag, I laughed as well. "Tom, you have no idea how light I'm traveling," I said.

Reaching into his shirt pocket, Tom said, "Mr. McLelland wanted me to be sure I gave you my card. If you ever need transportation to anywhere, give me a call, day or night."

Taking the card, I put it in my pocket.

"Thanks again Tom," I said, as I turned and headed to the door.

I reached under the ledge of the table, sitting on the patio and retrieved the hidden key. Unlocking the door, I stood for a moment before entering. Once inside, I looked around the kitchen and then I took the few steps into the living room. My leg was throbbing and my shoulder ached, but it was great being home. I sat down on the sofa thinking about what I was going to have for dinner.

I woke up the next morning as the sun was beginning to creep through the window. I didn't even remember falling asleep. I laughed when I realized I still had the Sears and Roebuck bag in my lap. I sat very still listening to the silence of the morning as it slowly inched its way into my house.

I rose and walked into the kitchen to take stock of the few supplies I had stored away. Thank goodness I had coffee. After getting the coffee pot going, I started looking for something to eat. Rummaging through my emergency food I finally settled on a can of chili and some crackers...a hearty breakfast for sure. Once I finished eating, I made a mental note to compile a grocery list and make a run to the store. I was walking a lot better, less limping. However, I was still having issues with my shoulder. My shoulder hurt, but the main issue was using my arm. My eye/hand coordination was bad and I had difficulty lifting even the slightest of weight.

After finishing my 2nd cup of coffee, I reached for a pen and paper. I knew if I wanted to get myself back into shape, it had to start now. I spent over an hour mapping out an aggressive exercise/rehabilitation program. I knew I had to start out slow. I planned some activities for each day. On the days I rested some parts of my body, I worked other parts.

Chapter 20 - Rehabilitation

I spent the next 6 months working on my rehabilitation. It began with a half a mile walk each morning and evening. Eventually I started a slow jog, then a light run. Over time the half a mile became a mile. I would run 2 days and then rest on the third day. By the end of the 6 months, I was doing two, 5 mile runs a day.

I followed the same routine with my shoulder/arm. Working with very light weights, two days on then a one-day break. I gradually increased the weight. Over time, I increased the workout to twice a day. By the end of the 6 months, I was bench pressing 180 lbs. and doing 100 push-ups 3 times a day. For a weightlifter, this accomplishment isn't impressive. But, as 6 months ago I barely could lift a coffee cup, I was pleased.

Over the course of my rehabilitation, Clay had called numerous times inquiring about my progress. I learned he had, for all practical purposes, given up his position at his dad's company. He went on to say, officially, he was still employed. But it was completely for appearances. Clay never said what he was doing. There are some things you don't discuss over the phone. However, I was pretty sure I knew.

On two separate occasions I spoke with Senator Dial. I initiated the first call to explain my sudden departure from the hospital. Dial said he understood. We discussed my future to some extent. It was decided I should apply for retirement. Senator Dial assured me, if I ever desired to return, there would be a job waiting.

The second time I spoke to Senator Dial, it was he that contacted me. He informed me my paperwork had been processed and approved. I was now officially retired from the employment of the United States government. He also arranged for someone to send me a brochure of information and benefits pertaining to my new status. He thanked me again for saving his life, just as I thanked him for all he had done for me. We both felt a bit uncomfortable. Before ending the call, Dial did let me know, Colonel Mathew expressed a desire to speak with me. I let the Senator know I still had the Colonel's number. Senator Dial thanked me one last time before ending the call.

I sat there for a few minutes thinking about my future. I picked up the phone and called Colonel Mathews. That phone call set my life on a path far beyond anything I could have expected.

After several months of covert training, I started working for the Colonel's operation. I became part of a small group of former military individuals traveling throughout different parts of the world in various fact-finding missions. In the realms of military jargon, we did Recon work.

Reconnaissance: aka Recon:

Trying to get an advantage over your enemy by means of spying or unobserved surveillance goes back to the beginning of time. All armies had "Scouts." These "Scouts" would operate forward of the military units, securing information of the enemy. At the time, this information consisted primarily of location and strength of the opposing armies. With the advent of aircraft, first hot air balloons, and later airplanes, recon consisted of gaining elevation to observe the enemy.

Early during WWII, the military of the day started perfecting this policy. Following the example of the British and Germans, the US Marines developed the first true Reconnaissance units. During the Vietnam war, all branches of the military activated units specializing in Recon.

Creed

Realizing it is my choice and my choice
alone to be a Reconnaissance Marine, I
accept all challenges involved with this
profession. Forever shall I strive to maintain
the tremendous reputation of those who
went before me.
Exceeding beyond the limitations set down
by others shall be my goal. Sacrificing
personal comforts and dedicating myself to
the completion of the reconnaissance
mission shall be my life. Physical fitness,

mental attitude, and high ethics—The title of Recon Marine is my honor.

Conquering all obstacles, both large and small, I shall never quit. To quit, to surrender, to give up is to fail. To be a Recon Marine is to surpass failure; To overcome, to adapt and to do whatever it takes to complete the mission.

On the battlefield, as in all areas of life, I shall stand tall above the competition. Through professional pride, integrity, and teamwork, I shall be the example for all Marines to emulate.

Never shall I forget the principles I accepted to become a Recon Marine. Honor, Perseverance, Spirit and Heart.

A Recon Marine can speak without saying a word and achieve what others can only imagine.

"Swift, Silent, Deadly"

Chapter 21 - The Team

As the plane moved through the dark night, I contemplated the goals of this mission. There's no such thing as a normal or routine mission. Realistically, this should be nothing but a trek to the designated zone, a quick look around, compiling the requested information, a hike back to the extraction point and a long ride home. In reality, it could be that simple or it could become complex.

As I pondered the many aspects of this endeavor, I looked over this group of soldiers. Each man is trained in one of several specific areas. Communications, Weaponry, Hand to Hand Combat, Medical, Language and Local customs. Outside of their specialty, they are all cross trained extensively in the other areas, to the point that each man is capable of doing his job and that of another.

Clay's specialty is weaponry. He has an elevated skill level in radio communications. He understands how terrain can affect radio transmission, plus he can build a "makeshift" antenna out of a beer can. He's proficient in four different languages.

Tony Danley. Like Clay, Tony has a vast understanding of military radios. He not only speaks Spanish; he speaks it with a street dialect. He knows the slang and cuss words to use when appropriate. Tony holds a First-Degree Black Belt and several other martial arts degrees. Before joining up with Colonel Mathews, Tony worked as a private contractor, teaching Hand to Hand Combat techniques to military officers going through survival training.

Tom Brookfield. Tom's baptism under fire was as a medic in Vietnam. He was wounded twice and awarded the Bronze Star for his unselfish actions during the Hamburger Hill action while serving with the 101st Airborne. After his discharge, Tom attended medical school for a couple of years. He's also a small arms specialist.

Keith Phillip Carroll. No one dare call him by his given name. To the few friends he has, he's KP. KP speaks so many different languages, I can't keep up with them all. KP is a native Indian from the New

Mexico, Arizona area. In addition to the multi-world languages, he speaks four different Indian dialects. His ability to track humans or animals through dense terrain is nothing but amazing.

Cliff Rush. Cliff is a quiet, unassuming person. Some have made the mistake of viewing his quiet demeanor as passiveness. Cliff loves to fight. I wouldn't consider him a hand-to-hand expert. He has more of a street fighter's approach, but with the agility and quickness of a cat. More than once he has squared off with a more skilled fighter, only to come out the victor. Cliff was a sniper in Vietnam. Story has it, if he hadn't been wounded from a mortar blast, he possibly would have topped Carlo Hathcock's record of confirmed kills.

Howard Andrews. At 6'8", over 300 lbs., Howard stands out. However, it's not just his size that causes everyone to take note of Howard. He has a look in his eyes that causes fear in the average man. He's very light on his feet, moving like a man much smaller. His size and weight combined with his agility makes him a force to be dealt with in hand-to-hand combat. Howard has a reputation for not getting along with people in authority. I learned early on, once the command to "Lock and Load" is given, Howard knows no equal when it comes to being a soldier.

It was raining as the plane made its landing approach. I'm always amazed at the pilots in these amphibious crafts. How do they know where to land? There's not an airport, just a huge body of water! The landing was choppy and we felt the waves as the pilot guided the plane into a small cove. It was obvious he had been here before. It was just after midnight when the plane came to a stop. We started gathering our gear as two small boats pulled up to the side door of the plane.

Once on shore, we were directed to a small warehouse. As I entered the two large sliding doors, I was greeted by a slightly overweight man with a half-smoked cigar in his mouth. "You must be Captain Allison," he said. "I recognize you from the photograph in your file."

"Yes, I'm Byron Allison," I replied. I find it odd; I'm always addressed by my former rank even though I haven't been in the military for several years.

"Captain, my name is Jones," the cigar smoking dude continued. "Not Mr. Jones, just Jones. I'm here to help you boys get ready. We have a place for you and your crew to get some rest, eat a bite and prepare to leave just after dark tomorrow." As he gestured toward the far end of the warehouse, Jones continued. "Back there you will find bunks, bath facilities and we have a small grill with someone available for the time you folks will be visiting. Also, Captain you and I need to sit down and go over a few details. But that can wait until you and your men get settled."

I thanked Jones and motioned for the men to follow me. Once we were in the bunk area, I gathered the crew together.

"OK guys listen up," I started. "We will be here until tomorrow night. First thing, clean and check your weapons. Then I suggest we all get some sleep. This might be the last night of decent rest for a few days. We leave tomorrow night just after dark. Once I have more information on the departure, I will go over the mission details with everyone. Tony, you are in charge of radio communications. Once you get the radio, you, Clay and I will go over the frequencies and make sure we are synched with the extraction team. Get your weapons in order and try to get some rest."

I walked back to my bunk, retrieved my cleaning kit from my bag and started cleaning my rifle. Once satisfied my rifle and pistol were ready for what may come, I stretched out on the bunk.

No one set a wake-up call. No one set an alarm. No one had to. It was getting close to kick-off time and everyone's height of awareness had increased ten-fold. By daylight everyone was stirring around. I could smell bacon frying back in the grill. After a breakfast of bacon, eggs, sausage gravy poured over biscuits, every man went their separate way. Some were checking their gear one more time, others reading, the remainder just lying in their bunks. Every warrior has his own way of mentally preparing. These guys are no different.

Clay and I were going over the terrain maps when a tall skinny fellow approached. "Captain," he said. "Jones has asked if you and Mr. McLelland will join him upstairs in the office." The guy motioned to some stairs off to our left. "Jones said to bring your maps too." With that, he turned and walked away.

Clay gathered the maps and we headed up the stairs. At the top of the stairs was a small landing. Just to the left was a large window allowing a view of the whole warehouse. To the right was a window unit air conditioner. Just as I started to knock, I heard a voice from inside shout, "Come in". Opening the door, Clay and I walked in. The room was like a meat locker. The air conditioner was certainly doing its job. Behind a desk sat Jones, with a half-smoked cigar in his mouth. I wondered if it was the same one from last night.

"Byron, Clay, if I can address you by your names," said Jones. Before we could reply, Jones stood up and walked around the desk while reaching into his shirt pocket. He continued, never removing the cigar from his mouth.

"Boys, it's a tradition of mine to have a cigar and a drink of good whiskey before I start a mission. A habit I started back in Nam. I hope you two will join me." I hadn't noticed the three glasses of whiskey sitting on the edge of the desk.

"These are the best Cubans cigars ever rolled," Jones said, as he handed one each to Clay and I.

He pulled a tip cutter and lighter from his pants pocket and laid them on the desk. After cutting the tips and lighting our cigars, Clay and I picked up the half-filled glasses. Without hesitation, Jones lifted his glass.

"Here's to peace, love, prosperity and a safe trip home," Jones said, as we clinked our glasses together. With that, we all took a hearty slug of the whiskey.

Jones continued, "Sit down gentlemen, let's enjoy the cigar and the remainder of our drink before we get down to business." We made small talk for the next 10 minutes before Jones set his empty glass on the desk.

"Gents, tonight just after dark," Jones began, "two small boats will take you and your crew on an hour trip to the mainland." Jones made a notation with his finger to a spot on the map. "You will be dropped off here. Your objective is here." He made another notation with his finger.

"I realize I'm not telling you anything you haven't already been briefed on. I just wanted to be sure we are on the same page. With luck, this will be a simple reconnaissance mission. Get in, look around, and get out. However, we do have a few contingency plans should things go to hell. If you will notice on the map, there are two areas marked LT Green and LT Blue. These are helicopter pick up points. Understand, for us to put a chopper in the air, is tantamount to invading a sovereign nation."

Jones laughed before continuing. "Of course, sending you guys in is just as risky. My point here is, if shit hits the fan, we will get you guys out. My communications people are meeting with your guy to ensure we have all the frequencies synched. Good luck gentlemen and I hope to see all of you back here in a few days. I will have fresh cigars and a new bottle of whiskey waiting."

Clay and I stood, shook hands with Jones and headed down the stairs. I gathered the team together one last time.

"OK guys," I started, "None of you are newbies. We've all done this type of mission before so I won't bore you with the newbie speech. I do expect everyone to stay alert, do your job and let's make this as non-eventful as possible. Does anyone have any questions?"

No one made a sound.

"OK," I continued, "we will be boarding a couple of small boats right after dark. Approximately 1950 hours. Be secured and ready no later than 1900 hours. Chow will be served at 1800 hours in the grill area. If there's nothing else, let's get ready to earn our pay."

That last statement drew a laugh. The remainder of the day slowly ticked by. I noticed some of the team playing cards. Mostly, everyone just laid around.

The guy operating the grill had a large platter of hot dogs waiting when I arrived. Maybe it was just the circumstances, or maybe not, but these were the best hot dogs I've ever eaten. I heard the cook tell someone he was a hot dog chef and these were his gourmet dogs. I wasn't the only one that liked these gourmet hot dogs. By the time we finished, the cook had prepared two additional platters. I saw Hal walk by and grab the last one.

Slowly, one by one, everyone headed back to their bunk. It was time to get serious. Camo face paint was pulled from each rut sack and applied. Weapons were checked and re-checked. Clothes, boots, webbing and packs were double checked.

I gave a quick shout, "Ready." Each man, one by one replied the same. It was time to board the boats.

Chapter 22 - The Mission Begins

The hour boat ride to the mainland, as described by Jones, was just that. It was 58 minutes from the time the boats shoved off to when we touched the beach. The beach was sandy with areas of rocks cropping out. The boats pulled us to one of the rock formations jetting out from the sandy shore.

As I eased over the side of the boat, into a foot of water, one of the boat crew laid his hand on my shoulder and whispered, "See you in two days, be safe." I raised my thumb as I made my way to the shore.

The team had made their way up the sandy slope. Clay and Tony were looking to our front as Hal and Cliff covered our flank. I wanted to give the boats time to get far enough out so they couldn't be seen. I also wanted to wait and let our ears, eyes and senses adapt to the new surroundings. The terrain here was relatively flat, sandy and littered with scrub bushes.

We had approximately 4 miles before we hit the jungle and didn't want to be caught in the open after daylight.

After taking a quick glance at my compass just to get my bearings, I leaned over, whispering, "KP, take point. Hal, you bring up the rear. Everyone else knows what to do. Keep about 10 feet between you and the one you are following."

(Order #6 of the STANDING ORDER ROGER RANGERS, issued by MAJOR ROBERT ROGERS in 1759 states;
When we're on the march we march single file, far enough apart so one shot can't go through two men.)

"Standard patrol procedures, hand signals only. If anyone needs to piss, do it now. We will stop again in about an hour. Let's move out."

Without a word, each man took up his position, except Hal, who decided he needed to pee first. The night was ideal for a patrol. It was calm and still. You could hear the night sounds. There was just enough ambient light to see 20 to 30 feet on all sides. Covering the 4 miles before daylight shouldn't be an issue.

I figured we covered just over a mile and a half the first hour. I called for a break-in-place. You never want your force bunched. I eased my way up to KP's position. Whispering, I made sure he was OK on point. I knew before he answered what his reply was going to be. "Yes sir," he said, "I'd rather be in the front than the rear".

After about 15 minutes I signaled for everyone to move out. As the column started moving, I waited for

Hal. Like with KP, I quietly inquired. Hal never gives a straight answer if he doesn't have to. I asked if he was OK in the rear. His reply didn't surprise me.

"Hell Captain, I'm used to being in the back of the bus." He then snickered, laid his hand on my shoulder and continued. "I got our backs, sir, don't worry about me."

I nodded and moved back to the column.

About 45 minutes into our second hour, Clay suddenly signaled for everyone to stop. As is procedure, each person signals the one behind and everyone takes a defensive, kneeling position. I crouched and moved my way up to Clay, who motioned up to KP. Still crouching, I quietly moved to his position. Once there, I found KP lying on his side. With hand signals, he indicated he heard something. Then with a soft whisper, he said, "Voices, I hear human voices. Maybe 50 yards up the trail."

In the briefings I clearly remember being told, there wasn't any known reason for anyone to be here. So much for intel.

By now, Clay had crawled his way to our position. Signaling Clay to hold his position, I nudged KP and he and I started a slow crawl forward. The sounds got louder as we got closer. Finally, we were able to see five men with shovels digging in the sand. Sitting beside the men was a wagon being pulled by a pair of mules. The first thought that crossed my mind was a mass grave. Were these men digging a hole to bury bodies? It didn't make sense they would be digging graves. Then I realized what they were digging. They were filling sandbags. Two men were holding the bags, as two others were shoveling sand into them and the fifth guy was loading them on the wagon. I calculated the wagon to be about ¾ full. I signaled KP to hold this position while I crawled back to the column.

Once back to Clay's location, I whispered, "Slight delay, hold your position, will explain."

He nodded and started a slow crawl to inform the others. I quietly made my way back to KP. After a very intense 30 minutes, the sandbag detail loaded their shovels and moved out. Waiting another 10 minutes, I assembled the team. Satisfied the sandbag detail was long out of ear shot I addressed the men.

"We stumbled upon a detail of five men and a mule drawn wagon filling sandbags. That raises the question. What is going on that requires sandbags? As we all know, sand bags are used for fortification purposes. Best I could tell, none of the men were armed. That indicates they didn't anticipate anyone else being out here. Which is a good thing. We don't have the time to trail the men. For now, we will assume they are headed to the same area we are. In the absence of good solid intel, we will also assume they are out here in the open at night for the same reason we are. They don't want to run the risk of being seen. They probably know there's high altitude reconnaissance. We will keep moving along our planned route and should be in the bush in another hour. KP, stay on point and everyone stay alert."

The next hour was uneventful. I could tell we were getting closer to thicker vegetation. The ground was starting to get harder. The sand was slowly giving way to firmer soil. Small trees and clumps of bushes replaced the waist high grass. Within a half a mile of leaving the grassy area we were in what would best be described as a rainforest. The further inland we went, the thicker the overhead canopy became. As we moved forward, we lost what ambient light we had. We were still a few hours away from day break. I decided this would be a good place to stop. I eased my way up to KP.

"Find a slight clearing we can hold up. I don't want to stumble into another detail of workers." KP nodded and slipped out of sight.

As each man passed by, I relayed the information. I joined Hal and we didn't go more than 100 yards before we caught up with the team.

"Everyone try to get some rest," I whispered. "We will be here until daylight."

Slowly and quietly, each man removed his pack and sat on the damp ground. With the overhead growth so thick, ambient light is slow. Once rays of light penetrated the trees, I signaled everyone to start gearing up.

"Cliff, move up 50 yards or so," I said, "and make sure it's all clear. We will wait." Cliff gave me a thumbs up and moved forward. Ten minutes later, he returned with an all clear. I directed Cliff to stay on point and motioned to Tony to bring up the rear. I calculated we weren't much more than four miles from our assigned area of operation.

Chapter 23 - Mission Changes

It was approaching mid-day when we smelt it. A faint combination of smoke with a lingering acid taste. At the first hint of something being out of place, Cliff stopped and waited for us. We all knew this wasn't a natural scent and had to be man-made. Taking a few minutes to try and sort out a general direction of the odor, I instructed everyone to hold up here. I motioned Tony up to my position.

"Tony," I whispered, "you and I are going to move up and try to get a feel for what's ahead, since we know so little at this point. Clay, you take the others and set up a wedge perimeter. In case Tony and I get into trouble, everyone moves forward until we meet up. Tony, leave the radio and pack here. We want to move very quietly."

As Clay directed the others, Tony and I started our slow trek forward. The farther we moved, the stronger the smell became. About 100 yards in, we started hearing voices. Faint at first, but becoming more distinct the closer we got. I signaled Tony to hold up. We both listened in an attempt to make out their conversation. In the dense underbrush, we were able to get close enough to make out 4-5 men working in and out of a tent. The tent was open on both ends and had some form of a stove or device that required a pipe to exhaust smoke. I motioned to Tony to move back. Once out of sight of the tent, we returned to the team.

I sat down beside Clay and took out my map marking the location.

"I believe we have located a drug lab," I said to Clay. "But it has to be more than just a 4–5-man operation. I want to move past this part and try to determine the overall scope of what we have discovered."

Putting my finger on the map, I continued. "I want you to take Hal, Cliff and Tom and move around this side," drawing a semicircle with my finger.

"I will take the others and come around the opposite side. Don't go too far this first time.

Depending on the size of the compound, we may have to make several patrols. But for now, let's just try to get an idea of what we are faced with."

KP, Tony and I started out towards where we first saw the tent, making sure we stayed out of sight of the workers at the tent. We worked our way farther up the compound. Once we got past the tent area, we moved closer in. What we saw was cause for concern. The compound appeared to be divided into two areas. The lower part had several identical tents with smoke coming from the makeshift stacks. The upper area resembled more of a military encampment. We were able to observe 10-12 individuals in camo fatigues carrying various firearms. The military personnel, though armed, didn't seem to be concerned with the possibility of any type of intervention. We didn't observe any type of outposts or guard towers.

As we moved forward, we saw a small barbed wire fenced stockade. Inside were three men. These men appeared to be dressed in civilian attire. Their clothes were tattered and dirty. The stockade was guarded by two armed soldiers. I motioned to Tony and KP to start moving back to our rally point. I quickly marked this location on my map and followed.

We reached the rally point a few minutes before Clay and his team arrived. Once everyone was together, I instructed the team to set up a wedge position and stay alert.

"Clay," I whispered, "follow me." Clay and I moved farther away to make sure we couldn't be heard inside the compound. Once I felt satisfied that we were outside of hearing range, I stopped and pulled out my map. I was anxious to hear what Clay and his team had observed.

Clay retrieved his map and started to outline his findings. "We circled around to here," Clay started, as he indicated on his map. "At first, we noticed several of the tents. Once past them we started noticing sandbag bunkers. Some were completed and others were in various stages of completion. I counted 10 finished and 8 under construction. In between the tents and bunkers, we saw two buildings. One appeared to be barracks and the other, if I had to guess, was the headquarters and communication. There was a radio tower erected next to this building."

Clay had each structure noted on his map. He continued, "We counted 10 workers in and around the tents and 12 armed, uniformed men around the bunkers. Outside two of the bunkers were stacks of boxes. Military boxes, I assumed to be arms and ammo. Some of the men were carrying these boxes into the bunkers. There wasn't any type of perimeter nor did I observe towers.".

I went over what we had seen and went into detail about the stockade and the three men inside.

"What is your take on this?" I asked Clay.

"As I see it," Clay replied, "it's a drug operation protected by and possibly sponsored by some facet of the military. Now, the three men you saw in the stockade are a different matter. They don't fit into this scenario."

"Unless", I said, "they are some high-level individuals being held for ransom. The ransom doesn't necessarily have to include money. Although, it's not uncommon for members of a well to do family to be kidnapped. The part of that idea that doesn't fit, is the fact that all three of these men seem to be in the same age range. Kidnapping three members of the same family seems odd."

Clay and I sat for a few moments in silence contemplating what we had observed. I broke the silence.

"From a recon standpoint, we have completed this mission. We have the data. Location, size, and equipment. But I feel the presence of the three men requires further investigation." Clay nodded his head in agreement.

"Breaking radio silence at this juncture of this operation goes against protocol," I said. "However, I feel it warrants passing this information on before we pull out." Again, Clay nodded in agreement.

"When we get back to the rally point," I continued, "I'll take Tony and the radio and move back and see if we can make contact with Jones. They can decide our next move. Based on what we have observed, so far, I doubt they will be running any type of radio signal searches. However, if you see any type of unusual activity inside the compound, start pulling back. We will meet up with you here." I indicated a point on the map.

Clay and I gathered up our maps and headed to the rally point. Once there, I told Tony to get the radio and follow me. We moved back in the direction we came, but were careful not to follow our original path. Getting a radio signal under this thick canopy can be difficult. Tony kept looking at the overhead growth until he found a small overhead clearing.

"This looks like as good an area as we are going to find," Tony said.

"OK," I replied, "see if you can raise someone on the radio."

Tony turned the set on and gave it a minute to warm up. Adjusting the radio to an assigned frequency, he keyed the mic.

"Cinderella, Cinderella," Tony spoke into the mic. "This is King Arthur, I repeat, this is King Arthur. Over."

Someday, I would like to meet the people that make up these radio calls. They must have a fantastic sense of humor.

The radio was silent. I saw a worried look on Tony's face. "Cinderella, Cinderella, this is King Arthur. Over," Tony tried again.

Just as I was about to give up hope, the radio came alive. "King Arthur, King Arthur this is Cinderella, we have a 5/5 signal, Over" came the reply over the radio. Tony handed me the mic.

"Cinderella, please copy, 616075, I repeat 616075, Over." I replied. The number I first transmitted was an authorization code identifying me. This is used in the event the radio is captured or someone other than myself was attempting to use it.

"King Arthur, we acknowledge 616075, proceed with your transmission," came the reply.

I started my transmission with the details we had gathered, outlining the layout of the compound, the tents, bunker, number of workers and military personnel. I gave the information on the military boxes and their descriptions. Then I started laying out the details of the stockade.

"We observed three males, of medium build, possibly Hispanic, dressed in tattered civilian clothing. I would guess their ages to be mid to late 40's. The three men were being held captive in a small wired compound with armed guards. Their physical condition appeared to be good, Over."

There was a longer than expected delay before the radio crackled. "King Arthur, it's requested you hold your position until we can make some inquiries. Next radio contact schedule for 1600 hours. How copy, over."

"Roger, Cinderella, next radio contact, 1600 hours", I confirmed. The radio went silent. I motioned to Tony and he turned the radio off.

I gathered my map as Tony secured the radio and we headed back to the rally point. Once we arrived, I advised Clay on my talk with Cinderella. It was just past 1300, so we had 3 hours to kill.

"Clay, I want you to take your team and recon the area we covered earlier," I said, "and I will take my team and look over the other. Perhaps we will see something the other missed. Plus, I want each team to get a feel for the whole compound."

Hesitating for a moment, I continued. "Pay close attention to details. Start developing a plan for a raid. I'm not saying it's going to come to this, but I wouldn't be surprised if we are requested to attempt to rescue the captives."

At the mention of a raid, I saw the whole team react. Requesting a raid brings on a whole new dimension to this operation. These guys signed on expecting a recon mission. I know this crew and had no doubt they would follow whatever orders came from above. However, it would be within their rights to refuse. In a situation like this, it's an all or none endeavor. If one man balks, it's a no go.

Without a word, Clay and his team gathered their gear and headed out. We did the same.

Easing up the area Clay and his team explored earlier, I wanted to pay close attention to the

Headquarters building and especially the radio room. Disabling their ability to communicate with the outside world would be top priority.

"Tony," I whispered, "what would it take to bring down the antenna tower?"

Tony raised a small pair of binoculars to his eyes for a moment before replying.

"The tower appears to be made of wood. Bamboo I suspect. The fastest way would be to use a small bit of C4, plastic explosive. A well-placed volley of bullets might do it. The bullets would be noisy."

I was surveying the Headquarters building when we heard the sounds of vehicles, as two military trucks entered the main gate. The trucks stopped close to the sandbagged bunkers. Two men exited each truck as a couple of others lowered the tail gate. One man jumped into the bed of the truck and started dragging military style boxes to the rear while the others stacked them. All together, they unloaded 30 boxes of what could only be assumed was military armament. Whatever it was, this small group had enough weaponry to supply a large army. Once emptied, both trucks exited the compound the same way they entered. I signaled to my team and we headed back to the rally point. Clay and his team were waiting.

Clay had his map open and was making some notations. He motioned for me to come over.

"We saw the stockade," he began. "It appears one of the captives is moving around with a limp. Perhaps with a leg injury. By my observation, he would be slow getting around. Something to know in case of an escape. We witnessed a changing of the stockade guards. Very informal. Two guards arrived and the other two left. Military discipline is very nonchalant or non-existent. I spied one guy I took to be an officer. I couldn't make out his rank, but given his appearance and age, I suspect he might be in charge. We heard and saw the trucks enter, but weren't in a position to see where they parked."

I brought Clay up to date on the Headquarter building and the possibility of taking out the tower. I also filled him in on the truck activities. It was time for Tony and me to head back to the area we used for the radio.

We arrived at 1550 hours. Tony turned the radio on, checked the batteries and adjusted the frequency. At precisely 1600 hours, the radio came to life.

"King Arthur, King Arthur, this is Cinderella, how copy, over."

Taking the mic I replied, "Cinderella, this is King Arthur, 726045, I repeat, 726045. I copy loud and clear, over."

"King Arthur, this is Kid Galahad," the voice over the radio replied.

Where do they get these code names? I thought with a chuckle. I recognized the person talking. There's no hiding Colonel Mathews voice.

"We have a bit of an issue," the voice continued. "The three captives you described appear to be diplomatic dignitaries recently kidnapped. Their respective governments have requested we do whatever possible to gain their freedom. We also have reason to believe they will be moved or possibly executed tomorrow. In your professional opinion, what is the assessment of the situation, over."

I thought for a moment before responding. "With our limited resources," I started my reply, "the operation will be risky, but doable with minimum collateral damage, over."

I picked my words carefully. We came equipped for a recon mission and the possibility of a hot extraction. We weren't fully equipped for a raid.

"Arthur, I understand what you are saying," came the voice over the radio. "You and I have known each other for a while now and I value your opinion. Would you give this operation decent odds for success? If not, I want you and the team to pull out within the hour."

I was almost stunned by Mathew's response. It's against all operational protocol to be so personal in field radio communication.

I thought for a second before replying. "OK, consider it a go," I said. "Now let's discuss extraction. It's not likely we can eliminate all of the present threats. I expect we will be pursued and it's possible one of the captives is injured. Not critical, but his mobility is limited. Under good conditions we are several hours away from LT Blue."

"Affirmative, Arthur," Mathews replied. "We will have a team in place at LT Blue waiting. We will have armed birds in the sky about your location. What time frame do you expect to be operational? Over."

Mathews and I both knew gunships in this environment would be worthless. The canopy was so thick, they couldn't see anything and the chances of their armament penetrating the trees were slim. But it sounded good. I had already calculated the time frame. I quickly ran the numbers through my mind before replying.

"I plan to kick off at 0300 hours," I responded, "out no later than 0400 hours arriving at LT Blue, hopefully by 0600. Keep the communication line open, I will attempt to contact you with a report while on the move, over."

"Roger, Arthur", Mathew's voice replied over the radio. "I will see to things on this end. Good luck and be safe." The radio went silent.

"Captain," said Tony as he was securing the radio. "You mind if I make a suggestion?"

"Sure," I replied, "let me hear it."

"Sir, after dark, I believe I could walk into the compound without causing any suspicion. No one there seems to really be paying any attention. I possibly could place C4 on the tower with a timer. It's also possible I could move around to the stockade and warn the captives. The way I see it, if I'm detected, I'll start shooting and everyone can come to my rescue." He laughed as he picked up the radio.

"Tony," I replied, "let me talk with Clay and see how that would fit into our plans. If we go that route, and I think it has merit, I want one promise from you!"

Tony stopped in his tracks and turned to look at me.

"You have to promise," I continued, "you will not let anything happen to yourself. I made a promise to your dad." We both chuckled as we headed back to the rally point.

Once Tony and I reached the rally point, I signaled for everyone to gather around me. As they were huddling, I looked at Clay and said, "It's a go."

"OK men, here's the deal," I began. "This recon mission has changed. We are going to rescue the captives and destroy as much of the camp as possible. Rescue is our main goal. The more of the bad guys we can eliminate, the better our chances of making it to the extraction point. First, does anyone have a problem with the changes?"

The first thing I noticed was Hal's reaction. He never spoke a word, but the smile on his face told me all I needed to know. Cliff was the first to speak.

"Hell yeah," he said. "I was hoping for some action."

Tom and KP both replied with a thumbs up. I knew at that moment I had the right team for this job.

"After Clay and I work out the details," I continued, "we will give each man his assignment. For now, I want three men on guard and three resting. Tony and I will make one more recon patrol to check out the Headquarters building. Check your gear; each man should have a small packet of C4. Give what you have to Tony."

As the men started getting their gear ready, Clay and I pulled out our maps. I went over Tony's idea of infiltrating the compound. With a bit of reluctance, Clay agreed it was a good idea. Risky but good.

"If Tony has to go on the defensive," I began, "we will have lost the element of surprise. We go in blazing, a full assault. However, if he's successful, I want to just walk into the compound closest to the stockade and try to neutralize the guards and get the captives out unnoticed. Once the captives are secured and out of the compound, we will launch our assault. The dropping of the tower will be the first thing. Tony will set a timed charge on it and attempt to enter the radio room where he will set a charge on the radio. Everyone will have to be in position when the charges go off."

I took a breath and waited for Clay's response. Clay hesitated for a moment before giving me a thumbs up.

"I want Hal and Cliff to handle the stockade guards and secure the captives," I continued. "If the one injured captive can't walk, Hal can carry him and Cliff can cover their retreat. Tony and I will be on the back side. After he goes in, and all goes well, I will take part of the C4 and set them inside the bunkers. Hopefully, if there's ammo in the bunkers, they will ignite. You, Tom and KP take up positions just outside the barracks and neutralize as many as possible. Once the C4 goes off, we start falling back. You need to take out the generator as you pull back. Each group will exit in the areas they entered. We will meet at the original rally point to start our journey out of here. We kick off at 0300. I want to be out no later than 0400."

I picked up the map before continuing. "We are headed to LT Blue," I indicated on the map. "If things go really bad, getting the team out becomes the priority, if you understand what I'm saying."

Clay nodded before replying. "Let's hope that's not necessary, but I understand and agree."

"OK, get the guys together and we will go over the details and assignments." Clay gathered everyone and we explained the plan and each one's duties.

Chapter 24 - Rescue

At 0245 I made sure everyone was ready. I handed Tony a piece of paper. "Tony," I whispered, "once we start our retreat, I want you up front and moving ahead of us. As soon as you find a break in the canopy, turn the radio on and confirm you have made contact and then transmit this message."

The paper read, *mission complete, headed to home base.*

"Don't wait for a reply, turn the radio off and catch up with us. Leave the radio here, we'll pick it up on our way out."

"Yes sir," Tony replied

"OK guys, take up your position and I better see everyone's ugly faces back here in an hour."

With that we moved out.

When Tony and I reached our position, we both laid our rifles next to a large rock and pulled out our pistols and stuck them in our belts.

The compound was lit by an array of small lights strung around on poles. You could hear the generator running in the background. Tony casually started walking toward the Headquarters building. As he approached the steps leading up to the building, a man emerged. I eased my pistol out of my belt, knowing a shot from here would be worthless. Tony stopped and I could tell, they were exchanging words. Still being calm, I could see Tony gesturing with his hands. The man, not seeming to be excited, walked down the three steps to where Tony was standing. With one quick motion, Tony grabbed the man's arm, turning him sideways. In the same motion, Tony grasped the man's head with both hands and twisted. The now dead man never made a sound. I looked across the. compound as Tony dragged the lifeless body behind the building.

Tony came from behind the building as though nothing happened. He again walked to the steps and entered the building. Not seeing anyone, I made my way to the bunkers. Taking the C4 and a timer, I set charges in four of the bunkers with each timer set for 15 minutes. As I exited the bunker, I again saw Tony over by the radio tower setting a C4 charge.

While Tony and I were working on our assignment, Hal and Cliff entered the compound closest to the stockade as Clay, KP and Tom took positions by the barracks. One of the guards must have noticed Hal's size and attempted to challenge them. A short burst from Cliff's rifle took both of them out while Hal flung open the stockade's gate. The captives were standing and two of them made a move to the gate on Cliff's command. The third was slow to move, so Hal grabbed the guy and flung him over his shoulder. The two captives followed Hal carrying the third, as Cliff covered their retreat.

The blast of gunfire from Cliff woke up the camp. Men started running out the barracks door as Clay and his team opened fire. In the confusion, several came out unarmed. However, it didn't take but a few seconds until gunfire started emerging from the windows.

Tony and I quickly moved to the rear of the barracks as the back door swung open and men started running out. Without hesitation, Tony and I both started firing. There weren't any windows in the rear, only a small door. This made it difficult for them to effectively return fire. Realizing it was time for the C4 to start going off, Tony and I started our retreat. Tony was about 20 feet ahead of me, when a soldier came around the corner of the building. When he saw me, he hesitated. We were about 5 feet apart. For a brief moment, we just stood staring at one another. In that split second of time, I saw death in his eyes...a look I've seen before. It's as though you are seeing the depth of a man's soul. It's the moment a man knows he's about to die. The soldier tried to raise his rifle as I pulled the trigger. Death had claimed his soul. Turning, I quickly caught up with Tony.

We had just reached the spot we left our rifles, when the explosions started. We headed back to the rally point when I heard the generator die and saw the compound go dark.

Everyone made it out. I quickly assessed the situation.

"Is everyone OK," I asked.

"I've taken a round in the hip," Tom exclaimed.

Before I could reply he continued. "It's more in the ass than the hip," Tom went on. "I've checked it out. Nasty looking but minimal bleeding and I can move, just don't ask me to sit down."

"OK Tom," I replied. "Stay up front so we can keep an eye on you. Tony, grab the radio and get started. We will catch up. Cliff, take point, keep the two captives between you and Hal. Hal, you OK with carrying the other captive for now?"

Hal chuckled before replying. "Hell, Captain, I've carried heavier packs."

"Good, let's get moving. KP, you've got drag, keep your ears open and let me know if you detect anyone following."

"You got it, sir," KP replied.

As we started out, I glanced back toward the compound. All I could see was a bright orange glow. We were still hearing gunfire from the compound area. I wasn't sure if they were still firing or if rounds were going off in the burning bunkers.

We were moving slower than I wanted, but we were putting distance between us and the bad guys. At least that's what I thought. About 45 minutes into our journey, KP came up from the rear.

"Captain," KP said. "We have six guys behind us. They aren't trying to catch up, they are trailing us and radioing our location. I was able to get close enough to hear them giving location information."

"That can only mean one thing," I replied. "Someone is coordinating an ambush up ahead. KP, go up front and tell Cliff to hold up. Tell Clay to put everyone in a Line perimeter."

As KP moved forward, I pulled out the map and started looking for what might be a good ambush spot. If I were going to set up an ambush, where would I place it? After getting a feel for the terrain ahead, I joined the others.

I brought Clay up to speed on the situation. "We need to eliminate the force behind us," I explained. "If or when we walk into the ambush, I don't want to be hit from behind also and I suspect that's what they have in mind. I want you to take Tom, Hal and the captives and move forward some 300 yards. Just far enough that the captives will be out of danger. Keep an eye out for the forward ambush. However, I suspect they will be waiting here."

I pointed to a place on the map. "The terrain is more suitable and if I were setting up an ambush here's where it would be. Once we deal with the rear threat, we will join back up."

Clay nodded and started moving the captives, along with Tom and Hal, who was still carrying the injured captive.

I turned back to KP. "I want you to work your way to the left flank of the ones following us. When they reach here, we will have an ambush of our own setup. Once we engage, you will be in position to provide a flanking maneuver. Stay far enough back that you can catch anyone trying to withdraw. We will not be pursuing, so anyone you see is a bad guy. We need to take these guys out fast."

I knew, if anyone could track these guys undetected, KP was the one. With KP headed back into the bush I turned my attention to the remaining team.

"Cliff, you and Tony set up on the left of the trail. I will cover the right. Don't fire until I do. When you do fire, make it fast and hot. We need this over as quickly as possible."

We had barely gotten into position when we heard faint voices. My priority was the radio and radio operator. I anticipated he would be in the rear.

Five of the six men came into sight. It was obvious to me they didn't anticipate an ambush. The group was walking, somewhat in a casual manner, rifles flung over their shoulders. I waited as long as I could hoping the other man would enter the killing zone. Again, I assumed he would be the radio operator. I raised to my knee and fired a burst, aimed at the lead soldier. He never knew what hit him. At almost the same second I fired, Cliff and Tony opened up. The ambush was over in less than 10 seconds.

"Cliff!" I shouted, "You and Tony check the bodies for any papers." I doubted they would have anything of importance, but just wanted to be sure. As I stood, I heard a short burst of fire from down the trail. These guys were all carrying AK47s and it wasn't the sound of an AK I heard. It had to be KP firing and I was hoping he found the radio operator.

After a couple of minutes, KP came into sight. "Captain," he said, "I got the radio operator, but I'm not sure if he had time to report the ambush. He was either talking or trying to talk when I hit it. Either way, whoever was on the other end of the radio probably knows something happened."

"OK," I ordered, "we are done here. Let's catch up with the group."

We headed toward the others at a pretty good pace. Just as I expected, about 300 yards up the trail, waiting for us was the team.

All three captives were sitting on the ground. Clay told me he had sent Hal up the trail to keep an eye out. While waiting Tom had examined the injured captive and found his leg to be badly infected.

"Tom," I said, "how bad is the injury? Tom walked a bit closer before replying.

"His leg is bad. I applied some penicillin powder, but at this point, it's like putting a band-aid on a gunshot wound. The infection has moved up his leg and he's running a high fever. If we don't get him medical attention soon, I doubt he will make it. I detected what I suspect to be a piece of wood embedded. I didn't attempt to remove it. I just gave him a shot of morphine to ease his pain."

I realized the captive had not uttered a word.

"Tony," I stated, "go relieve Hal and get him back here. We need him to continue carrying the injured guy."

Tony turned and headed down the trail. In a couple of minutes, Hal appeared. "Hal," I addressed him, "you still OK carrying this guy? If not, we can rig up a litter."

"Naw Captain," Hal replied, "this dude ain't no problem."

We were about a mile from where I anticipated the ambush to be.

I turned my attention to KP. "KP, I want you to scout this area here." I indicated on the map.

"I want to first determine if in fact there's a force waiting," I continued. "If not, report back to me ASAP. If you do observe anything, get me as much intel as you can. I don't need to tell you, don't let them detect you. If you were to get in trouble, we might not be able to get there in time. Do a quick recon and get out. I want to give you about a 10-minute head start. You can move faster than we will be capable of. We will meet up here." Again, I fingered a place on the map.

"Once we have the intel", I continued, "we will plan our next move."

KP looked over the map for a second before heading out. I looked at my watch. After 10-minutes had passed I signaled everyone to get started.

"Cliff, you're back on point," I ordered. "Tony, stay close to me in case I need the radio. OK, keep your eyes open, let's go."

I could tell the captives were doing their best. At this point they were tired and not cut out for traveling in this terrain. One kept losing his shoe and having to stop to get his foot back in. We were moving a lot slower than I would have preferred. It took over an hour to cover the half mile trek. When we arrived at the designated meeting point, I was concerned KP wasn't waiting. I was about to send someone to search for him, when he came walking out of the bush. The first thing I noticed was his blood-soaked shirt. My thought was he had been wounded, until he spoke.

"Sorry to be so long getting back, Captain. Apparently, they had someone out doing their own recon. I didn't want to fire a shot and alert anyone, so I waited until I could get closer and used my knife."

I breathed a sigh of relief.

"You keep saying them," I replied. "I take it there's a force waiting?"

"Yes sir," KP continued. "Just like you had it figured. They are set up on that small slope shown on the map. I counted 20, but perhaps as many as 25 and they have at least one 30 caliber machine gun. They are not in a really good ambush formation. Just all lined up across the ridge."

Clay was standing beside me listening to KP's report.

"Thank,s KP," I said, "good work."

I laid the map out before addressing Clay. "OK, we are outnumbered and outgunned, but we might achieve the element of surprise. I realize it's dangerous to split our forces, but I was thinking about moving around each side and coming at them in a double flanking maneuver. If we can get in close enough, with their force in a line formation their sides will be exposed. Given the foliage, if we are careful, I think we can get in undetected. I'll take Tony and Tom and move to the left. You take Cliff and KP, and move to the right. Hal can stay back with the captives until we make our move. Leaving the captives back, Hal can move straight up the slope. By the time he starts his move, we should have their forces split. If they only have one machine gun, they can only bring it to bear in one direction."

Clay studied the map for a moment before commenting." As I see it, that's our only chance. The terrain of the flanking maneuver would give us a small advantage. At least we will be on the same level if not a bit higher. It sure beats coming head on into their position."

"OK, then we agree," I said with a smile. "Let's get the team together and go over the plan."

Clay went over the plans with the team. Each man knew his part in the operation. Hal asked how he would know when to start his move. Clay explained, as soon as we engage, he should start. We were all in agreement; we headed out.

We stayed together until we got about half way to our objective location. At that point we split with each team moving in their respective direction. Hal was instructed to give us a few minutes lead time. It was just as KP had reported. The ambush formation was in a straight line. The machine gun was located in the center pointing directly down the trail. I instructed Tom to concentrate his initial fire on the machine crew. I waited a couple of minutes to ensure Clay and his team were in position, then I fired.

Tom's aim was dead on; he hit both of the machine gun crew. Tony's fire was equally effective. Our first volley caused confusion and panic. When the ambush forces realized they were being ambushed their first reaction was to move. Unfortunately, they had nowhere to go. We had them pinned down. Their next reaction was as I hoped. The remaining force split, half turning to face us and the other half turned to face Clay and his team. By shafting as they did, the group that faced Clay's team were exposed to our line of fire and vice versa. Both of our teams were taking heavy fire, but the rate of attrition was on our side.

I heard Tony when he yelled, "I'm hit!"

I drew back and crawled to his position. He was lying on his back trying to get a bandage wrapped around his leg. Grabbing my knife, I ripped open the leg of his pants. The bleeding was substantial, but at a glance I was fairly certain an artery hadn't been hit. As I was trying to get the bandage on, he was trying to roll over and continue firing. I moved back to my original position and that's when I saw Hal. He walked up the middle of the trail like it was a Sunday walk. About 15 feet from the original ambush line, he emptied a 20-round clip up one side, reloaded and fired down the other side. That took all the fight out of the remaining few. This battle was over. Of the 23 members of this ambush squad, 18 were dead, 3 wounded and the other 2 just gave up.

Cliff grabbed Tony and started helping him down the slope. I signaled Clay and his team to join us. Hal reloaded and turned to go get the captives.

Noticing a bandage on Clay's arm, I asked "How bad?"

"Tom said it's just a scratch," Clay said with a laugh.

I turned to Tom and asked him, "How bad is it?"

"Really," Tom replied, "it just creased his arm. No muscle damage. Clay's lucky; another half an inch and it could have been serious."

Clay laughed again before commenting, "I get shot and Tom says I'm lucky."

This brought a chuckle from the remaining team.

Tom had Tony lay down so he could check his leg. "Tony," I heard Tom say, "your injury is not too serious. The round went straight through. Some muscle damage but nothing that won't heal in time. I can give you a shot of morphine, but we will need to put a litter together to get you out of here."

"We don't need a damn litter and I don't want a shot. Hand me one of those AKs and I'll just use it as a walking stick."

Cliff picked up one of the many AKs laying on the ground, removed the clip and cleared the chamber. He handed to Tony, "Here's your walking stick, my lord." Tony cursed, as he grabbed the stock of the rifle and pulled himself up.

By now Hal had made it back with the captives. KP walked over to me and in a whisper asked, "What do you want to do with these two?" Motioning to the two survivors of the ambush squad. I understood what he was asking.

I looked around before replying, "Grab a couple branches and let's put together a litter using webbing from these dead guys. The survivors can carry the injured captive and give Hal a break."

A couple of guys hastily rigged a litter and Hal placed the injured man in it. Tony, in words the survivors understood, explained. If either of them dropped the litter, both would be shot in the head on the spot. I saw both of them tighten their grip.

"We need to get going," I said. "We're not out of the woods yet, literally and figuratively speaking. Tony, can you still operate the radio?"

"Yes sir, I can," Tony replied. "Just not sure I can carry it."

Before I could comment, Hal walked over and picked up the radio, turned to Tony and said "Don't worry about carrying it, I got you covered."

"Before Hal walks off with it," I said, "get on the radio, and send this message."

I handed Tony a piece of paper that read:
Blooded, but not down. Will need medical assistance. Hope to arrive in less than 2 hours.

"Everyone else, saddle up!" As we started, I noticed Cliff helping Tony as best he could. We were slow, but we were moving. As soon as I felt sandy ground under my feet, I knew we were going to make it. LT Blue was close.

LT Blue was a small clearing just at the edge of the rainforest. We emerged from the thicket a few hundred yards short of the landing point. I saw three choppers on the ground and two gunships overhead. A medical crew with litters rushed out to meet us.

One of the choppers had the local government's flag on its side. The other two were black, and unmarked except for a small number on the tail. The two uninjured captives started going around thanking all the team members. It was then I realized, I had never heard either of them speak a word this whole time.

The three captives and two survivors were quickly loaded into their helicopter and took off. As the chopper was gaining altitude, I heard KP yell, "Look!" as he pointed toward the sky. I turned to see two bodies falling through the air. I wondered to myself if it wouldn't have been better to have taken KP up on his suggestion back in the bush. As soon as the medical crew looked over our wounded, we were loaded and out of that place.

Chapter 25 - Going Home

Clay, Tony and I climbed into the first chopper. The remainder of the team boarded the second. I heard Tom complaining when they laid him face down on a gurney. Tony was on a gurney stretched out between Clay and me. Once we gained enough altitude to feel safe, I looked over at Clay. He was sitting across from me with that shit-eating smile he is so famous for. He reached in his pocket and pulled out a pack of bent, twisted cigarettes. I leaned and took the pack from his hand, pulled two out, lit one and handed it to him. After lighting mine I took a deep breath.

When we landed back at the island, where all this began, I noticed a small, unmarked jet sitting on the tarmac. We were escorted into the warehouse. Tom was still complaining. Tom's gurney along with Tony's were carried in by the medical staff. Someone brought a wheelchair around and helped Tony into it. Before anyone could get to Tom, he rolled to his side and climbed to his feet.

"Dammit," Tom said, "I'm shot in the ass but I can still stand."

At the warehouse entrance were two men in Army uniforms. They asked if we would surrender all issued weaponry, ammo and any other issued equipment. We complied. Inside the warehouse was a large table set up. On the table were seven drink glasses half-filled with what I could only assume was whiskey.

As I was looking at the glasses, I heard Jones coming. I looked and there he was, with a half-smoked cigar between his teeth. I wondered again if this was the same one he had a few days ago.

"Byron," Jones started, "glad to have all of you back. I loved that message you sent. 'Blooded, but not down.' That is a classic. Anyway, we will have you boys out of here in a short time. We don't get many jets in here. But we wanted to get you boys off the island ASAP. The jet is being fueled. In the meantime, I have a drink of good Canadian Whiskey for each one of you brave soldiers."

Gesturing with his hand to a box on the table, Jones continued, "I also have some of the finest cigars this side of Havana. Help yourselves. There's plenty where those came from. The cook will have some of his gourmet hot dogs out in just a few minutes. I know you guys must be hungry. Wish we could do better, but out here in the middle of the Gulf our resources are limited."

Everyone, including myself, took Jones up on his offer. The whiskey burned going down, but it sure tasted good. I lit my cigar and realized Jones was right. It was one of the best cigars I'd had in a long time. Before I could compliment Jones on his choice of whiskey and cigars, he pulled me off to the side.

"I would like to see you and Clay in my office for a moment," he whispered. I turned and Clay was just lighting his cigar. He looked up and I motioned him to come with me as I followed Jones.

As we walked away, Jones loudly spoke up. "You boys drink up; we will be back in a few minutes."

We met the cook coming from the grill with a tray full of hot dogs. Clay and I each grabbed one as he passed. Once in Jones' office, his whole demeanor changed.

"Men," Jones started, "I wanted to be the first to say you guys did a fantastic job. The dignitaries you rescued would have never made it out alive. I regret to say, the injured one succumbed to his wounds. The local government has asked that we give each one of your team their heartfelt appreciation. You understand, they can't officially acknowledge your work, nor can we. It's a very thankless job we have. The jet will fly you guys back to the states. Once back in US territory, you will need to be debriefed. The wounded will be cared for as well. Under the circumstances, it might take a few days. I think you will find the accommodations agreeable."

With that, Jones stood up and headed for the door. We walked down the flight of stairs and discovered the warehouse was empty, with the exception of the cook.

"Everyone must be on the plane," Jones exclaimed. "You guys had best hurry, I wouldn't want you to miss the flight." He laughed.

Shaking our hands, Jones continued, "Take care men, it's a pleasure to have met both of you."

We thanked Jones and as we turned to head to the plane, the cook handed each of us two hot dogs.

The flight back to the States lasted less than two hours. This jet was a lot faster than the cargo plane we flew out on. After the whiskey and a stomach full of hot dogs, everyone was feeling good. The jet landed at a private airfield. To meet us were three ambulances, and three sedans. Tony was placed in one ambulance and Tom in another and reluctantly, Clay in the last. I inquired as to the destination of the wounded. The driver told me they would be taken to a private, on-site medical facility and once seen by the doctors, we would be able to visit. The remainder of us got into the sedans.

We were driven a short distance to what appeared to be a small hotel. There were no other vehicles present and I noticed we never left the airport compound. The lobby was small, with a counter on one side and a bar at the other. As we entered, we were greeted by the man behind the counter.

"Gentlemen," he stated, "welcome. I have a room waiting for each of you."

He called out each name and handed us a small envelope containing a key card.

Then he explained. "Once you get to your room, you will find a complete set of fatigues, including underwear and boots. Each room is actually a mini-suite with a small living room and a conference table. Once you've had a chance to shower and change, you will be brought a steak prepared to your liking. Inside the envelope is a dinner form. If you will be so kind, make your choices and leave it on the counter.

About that time, Colonel Mathews appeared. "Gentlemen," he began, "we are fully aware of the ordeal you've encountered these last few days and you are anxious to get home. Please bear with us. You will be compensated for your time. We want to give you some time to – how should I say it – decompress. Also, we have a few questions. We find it best to keep everyone isolated until we have time to talk. After dinner, someone will come to your room and go over a few questions. Once that's done, the bar will be open and everything is on the house. Tomorrow morning, we will have a group meeting and you will be given an airline ticket home. Any questions?"

No one spoke.

"Great." Mathews continued, "I will see everyone in the morning."

Everyone started filling out their food request form before heading to their room. Colonel Mathews approached me.

"Byron, I'll be up to your room in 2 hours. That should give you time to eat and clean up. By the way, great job."

He smiled and walked out the hotel door to a waiting car. I handed in my meal request and headed to my room. I showered and as I was putting on my new pair of fatigues, there was a knock on the door. I opened the door and a man rolled a tray in.

"Your dinner, sir," he said. "I hope you enjoy it."
He turned and closed the door behind him. I had barely finished when Colonel Mathews arrived. He didn't knock, he just spoke my name. I opened the door.

"I will make this short, Byron," Mathews said. "Just a couple of questions. The first, how did the men perform?" Before I could answer, Mathews continued, "If you had to go one another mission, is there any one of them you would not want on your team?"

I hesitated a moment waiting to see if he was going to ask another question.

"No sir," I began, "I would not hesitate to go with any of them. In fact, if I were to go on another mission, I would request each and every one."

"What about Howard Andrews?" Mathew asked. "I understand he can be difficult at times."

"Colonel," I replied, "Hal is as fine a soldier as I've ever served with. I understand he has had his issues, but in the field, he's everything I would want a team member to be."

"Good, great to hear," Mathews said. "I like to hear good things about my teams. One last question: You just said, 'if I were to go on another mission,' is there a chance this is your last?"

"Colonel", I said, "it's too soon for me to honestly answer that."

"I understand Byron," Mathews said. "Get some rest, I'm sure you need it. Oh, before I forget, I couldn't have asked for a better outcome on this mission. Granted you had a few walking wounded, but you and your team put down a possible coup and you did it with just six men. And to top that off, you rescued three civilians. Granted that one died, but he would have died regardless. At least his family can bury him. Your team will be down stairs at the bar in case you want to have a drink with them. Have a good evening, Byron and again, thanks for a great job."

"When can I see my wounded guys?" I asked.

"They need to get a good night's sleep," Mathews replied. "The group meeting will be at the medical facility in the morning; everyone will be there."

With that, Colonel Mathews got up and left.

As tired as I was, I wanted to go down to the bar for a few minutes. As soon as I stepped off the elevator, I heard them. Apparently, they finished sooner than I did. I walked around the corner to a loud round of applause. The first to greet me was KP.

"Captain," KP said, "I just want you to know, you are the best team leader I've ever served under."

I thanked him as Cliff was handing me a drink. "I believe you prefer Canadian blended whiskey, sir," Cliff said. "Yes, I do, but in a pinch, I'll drink about anything," I said with a chuckle.

Cliff lifted his glass and said, "Here's to Captain Allison, the best damn Captain to ever wear a pair of boots."

Everyone cheered.

I saw Hal as he came around the others. "Captain," Hal started, "I just want you to know, I would follow you through the gates of hell and never complain about the damn heat." Everyone raised their glass again and cheered.

"You guys are the best," I replied. "I couldn't find a better group to work with. It's been an honor, it truly has. Now if you don't mind, I'm headed to bed. I suggest you guys do the same."

I turned and headed back to my room.

The meeting the next morning was more of a reunion. The facility provided donuts and coffee. Tom was still bitching about having to lay on his stomach. They wouldn't let him get up.

I pulled up a chair beside Tony's bed. "How's the leg?" I asked

"It's OK." Tony replied. "They say I will need to be here for at least a week. Infection is the biggest threat. Afterwards, I'm told I will need some intensive rehabilitation and physical therapy, but in time I can expect full recovery."

"You are in luck," I said. "I know a place that specializes in just this type of rehab. I will write down the address and phone number and give it to you before I leave."

"Thanks," Tony said. "Captain, it was my pleasure to serve with you." "Tony", I replied. "The pleasure is all mine. Give my regards to your dad. Tell him my offer to take him fishing still stands."

"Yes sir, I will!" Tony stated.

I stuck out my hand and we shook.

I stood and walked over to Clay. "How's the scratch on your arm?" I asked with a chuckle.

Clay laughed before saying, "Hell, all I need is a Band-Aid and I can go home. Problem is, I can't convince the people here. They want to keep an eye on it for a few days. Then I'm headed back to California."

"Give my best to Clayton and your mom," I said. "If you get out my way, drop by, and I'll do the same if ever I'm on the west coast. Take care my friend."

We shook hands and I headed for the door. I had a plane to catch.

A Month Later

The moment I heard the car turn off the main road onto the dirt driveway leading to my house I knew who it was and why they were coming to see me. I also knew what my answer to their question would be.

I walked to the end of the porch and watched as two men stepped out of the car. It was obvious they had driven all night. They looked tired, clothes wrinkled, hair tousled. The driver exited the car and stretched for a moment. The second guy was a little slower getting out. He was walking with a cane.

I looked at both of them before speaking. "I was wondering when you two would get here. Anthony, you're looking good for an old retired Master Sergeant. Tony, before you say anything, I want you to know, I'm a bastard of a physical therapist but before we finish, you will be running marathons."

We all laughed.

In life, the most valuable asset a person possesses, next to health, is time. Taking your time to read my book is tantamount to you giving me a gift of your time. I sincerely appreciate this gift.

If you have any comments, please contact me at: Sterling849@yahoo.com

Terry Dailey

A Mercenary's Story is a fictional book. Any resemblances to individuals, incidences, locations or situations are purely coincidental.

No part of this book can be used, copied or altered in any way without the written consent of the author.

Made in the USA
Columbia, SC
26 July 2022

63857340R00102